"Don't tell me you're a..."

Gideon kept his eyes on the road as he spoke, trying hard to concentrate on his driving.

"No," Chris said quickly, resting her head against his shoulder. "But the sum total of my experience took place in the back seat of a '72 Chevy."

Gideon was amused by that. "I never did it in a car." Most everywhere else when he'd been younger, but never a car. "What was it like?" He pressed her hand on his thigh and held it there. "Wouldn't it be kind of cramped?"

"It just takes a little ingenuity...with positions." She was picturing the wildest things. "You have to be half on, half off the seat...."

He began moving her hand against his thigh, urging it back and forth. "Would we be undressed?"

Chris sucked in her breath. "If you wanted to, but it might be cold."

His voice was low, like liquid fire. "I'd want to do it, anyway. I want to see what you look like all over. Then I'd warm you up."

BARBARA DELINSKY

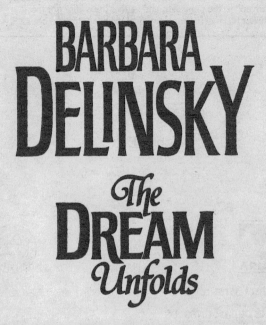

The DREAM *Unfolds*

MIRA BOOKS

MIRA

ISBN 1-55166-161-6

THE DREAM UNFOLDS

Copyright © 1990 by Barbara Delinsky.

MIRA and the star colophon are trademarks of MIRA Books.

Printed in U.S.A.

The DREAM Unfolds

1

They were three men with a mission late on a September afternoon. Purposefully they climbed from their cars, slammed their doors in quick succession and fell into broad stride on the brick walk leading to Elizabeth Abbott's front door. Gordon Hale rang the doorbell. It had been decided, back in his office at the bank, that he would be the primary speaker. He was the senior member of the group, the one who had organized the Crosslyn Rise consortium, the one who posed the least threat to Elizabeth Abbott.

Carter Malloy posed a threat because he was a brilliant architect, a rising star in his hometown, with a project in the works that stood to bring big bucks to the town. But there was more to his threat than that. He had known Elizabeth Abbott when they'd been kids, when he'd been the bad boy of the lot. The bad boy no longer, his biggest mistake in recent years had been bedding the vengeful Ms. Abbott. It had only happened once, he swore, and years before, despite Elizabeth's continued interest. Now, though, Carter was in love and on the verge of marrying Jessica Crosslyn, and Elizabeth had her tool for revenge. As chairman of the zoning commission, she was denying Crosslyn Rise the building permit it needed to break ground on its project.

Gideon Lowe was the builder for that project, and he had lots riding on its success. For one thing, the conversion of Crosslyn Rise from a single mansion on acres of land to an elegant condominium community promised to be the most challenging project he'd ever worked on. For another, it was the most visible. A job well-done there would be like a gold star on his résumé. But there was another reason why he wanted the project to be a success. He was an investor in it. For the first time, he had money at stake, *big* money. He knew he was taking a gamble, risking so much of his personal savings, but if things went well, he would have established himself as a businessman, a man of brain, as well as brawn. That was what he wanted, a change of image. And that was why he'd allowed himself to be talked into trading a beer with the guys after work for this mission.

A butler opened the door. "Yes?"

Gordon drew his stocky body to its full five-foot-ten-inch height. "My name is Gordon Hale. These gentlemen are Carter Malloy and Gideon Lowe. We're here to see Miss Abbott. I believe she's expecting us."

"Yes, sir, she is," the butler answered, and stood back to gesture them into the house. "If you'll come this way," he said as soon as they were all in the spacious front hall with the door closed behind them.

Gideon followed the others through the hall, then the living room and into the parlor, all the while fighting the urge to either laugh or say something crude. He hated phoniness. He also hated formality. He was used to it, he supposed, just as he was used to wearing a shirt and tie when the occasion called for it, as this one did. Still he couldn't help but feel scorn for the woman who was now rising, like a queen receiving her court, from a chintz-covered wingback chair.

"Gordon," she said with a smile, and extended her hand, "how nice to see you."

Gordon took her hand in his. "The pleasure's mine, Elizabeth." He turned and said nonchalantly, "I believe you know Carter."

"Yes," she acknowledged, and Gideon had to hand it to her. For a woman who had once lain naked and hot under Carter, she was cool as a cucumber now. "How are you, Carter?"

Carter wasn't quite as cool. Losing himself to the opportunity, he said, "I'd have been better without this misunderstanding."

"Misunderstanding?" Elizabeth asked innocently. "Is there a misunderstanding here?" She looked at Gordon. "I thought we'd been quite clear."

Gordon cleared his throat. "About denying us the building permit, yes. About why you've denied it, no. That's why we requested this meeting. But before we start—" he gestured toward Gideon "—I don't believe you've met Gideon Lowe. He's both a member of the consortium and our general contractor."

Elizabeth turned the force of her impeccably made-up blue eyes on Gideon. She nodded, then seemed to look a second time and with interest, after which she extended her hand. "Gideon Lowe? Have I heard that name before?"

"I doubt it, ma'am," Gideon said. Her hand felt as cool as that cuke, and nearly as hard. He guessed she was made of steel and could understand why once had been enough for Carter. He knew then and there that he wasn't interested even in once, himself, but he had every intention of playing the game. "Most of my work has been out in the western counties. I'm new to these parts." If he sounded like a nice country boy, even a little Southern, that was fine for now. Women liked that. They found it sweet, even charming, particularly when the man was as tall as Gideon was, and—he only thought it because, after thirty-nine years of hearing people say it, he supposed he had the right—as handsome.

"Welcome, then," she said with a smile. "But how did you come to be associated with these two rogues?"

"That's a damn good question," he said, returning the smile, even putting a little extra shine in it. "Seems I might have been taken in by promises of smooth sailing. We builders are used to delays, but that doesn't mean we like them. I've got my trucks ready to roll and my men champing at the bit. You're one powerful lady to control a group of guys that way."

Elizabeth did something with her mouth that said she loved the thought of that, though she said a bit demurely, "I'm afraid I can't take all the credit. I'm only one of a committee."

"But you're its chairman," Gordon put in, picking up the ball. "May we sit, Elizabeth?"

Elizabeth turned to him with a look of mild indignance. "Be my guest, though it won't do you much good. We've made our decision. As a courtesy, I've agreed to see you, but the committee's next formal meeting won't be until February. I thought I explained all that to Jessica."

At mention of Jessica's name, Carter stiffened. "You explained just enough on the phone to upset her. Why don't you go over it once more, face-to-face, with us."

"What Carter means," Gordon rushed to explain, "is that we're a little confused. Until yesterday afternoon, we'd been under the impression that everything was approved. I've been in close touch with Donald Swett, who assured me that all was well."

"Donald shouldn't have said that. I suppose he can be excused, since he's new to the committee this year, but all is never 'well,' as you put it, until the last of the information has been studied. As it turns out, we have serious doubts about the benefit of your project to this community."

"Are you kidding?" Carter asked.

Gordon held up a hand to him. To Elizabeth, he said, "The proposal we submitted to your committee went through the issue of community impact, point by point. The town has lots to gain, not the least of which is new tax revenue.''

Elizabeth tipped her head. ''We have lots to lose, too.''

''Like what?'' Carter asked, though a bit more civilly.

''Like crowding on the waterfront.''

Gordon shook his head. ''The marina will be limited in size and exclusive, at that. The price of the slips, alone, will discourage crowds.''

''That price will discourage the local residents, too,'' Elizabeth argued, ''who, I might add, also pay taxes to this town.''

''Oh, my God,'' Carter muttered, ''you're worried about the common folk. Since when, Elizabeth? You never used to give a damn about anyone or anything—''

''Carter—'' Gordon interrupted, only to be interrupted in turn by Elizabeth, who was glaring at Carter.

''I've moved up in the hierarchy of this town. It's become my responsibility to think of everyone here.'' When Carter snorted in disbelief, she deliberately looked back at Gordon. ''There's also the matter of your shops and their effect on those we already have. The town owes something to the shopkeepers who've been loyal to us all these years. So you see, it's not just a matter of money.''

''That's the most honest thing you've said so far,'' Carter fumed. ''In fact, it doesn't have a damn *thing* to do with money. Or with crowding the waterfront or squeezing out shops. It has to do with you and me—''

Gordon interrupted. ''I think we're losing it a little, here.''

''Did you expect anything different?'' Elizabeth said in a superior way. ''Some people never change. Carter certainly hasn't. He was a troublemaker as a boy, and he's a troublemaker now. Maybe *that's* one of the reservations my committee has—''

Carter sliced a hand through the air. ''Your 'committee' has no reservations. You're the only one who does. I'd venture to guess that your 'committee' was as surprised as we were by this sudden withholding of a permit. Face it, Lizzie. You're acting on a personal vendetta. I wonder what your 'committee' would say, or the townspeople, for that matter, if they were to learn that you and I—''

''Carter!'' Gordon snapped at the very same time that Gideon decided things had gone far enough.

''Whoa,'' Gideon said in a firm but slow and slightly raspy voice. ''Let's take it easy here.'' He knew Carter. When the man felt passionately about something, there was no stopping him. It had been that way with Jessica, whom he had wooed doggedly for months until finally, just the day before, she agreed to marry him. It was that way with Crosslyn Rise, where he had spent part of his childhood. Apparently it was that way, albeit negatively, with Elizabeth Abbott. But Gideon knew Elizabeth's type, too. Over the years, he had done enough work for people like her to know that the more she was pushed, the more she would dig in her heels. Reason had nothing to do with it; pride did.

But pride wouldn't get the consortium the building permit it needed, and the permit was all Gideon wanted. "I think," he went on in the same slow and raspy voice, "that we ought to cool it a second." He scratched his head. "Maybe we ought to cool it longer than that. It's late. I don't know about you guys, but I've been working all day. I'm tired. We're all tired." He looked beseechingly at Elizabeth. "Maybe this discussion would be better saved for tomorrow morning."

"I don't believe I can make it then," she said.

Gordon added, "Tomorrow morning's booked for me, too."

Carter scowled. "I have meetings in Springfield."

"Then dinner now," Gideon suggested. "I'm starved."

Again Gordon shook his head. "Mary's expecting me home. I'm already late."

Carter simply said, "Bad night."

Gideon slid a look at Elizabeth. "We could talk over dinner, you and I. I know as much about this project as these bozos. It'd be a hell of a lot more peaceful. And pleasant," he added more softly. "What do you say?"

Elizabeth was interested. He could see that. But she wasn't about to accept his invitation too quickly, lest she look eager. So she regarded him contemplatively for a minute, then looked at Gordon and at Carter, the latter in a dismissive way, before meeting Gideon's gaze again.

"I say that would be a refreshing change. You're right. It would be more peaceful. You seem like a reasonable man. We'll be able to talk." She glanced at the slender gold watch on her wrist. "But we ought to leave soon. I have an engagement at nine."

As announcements went, it was a bitchy one. But Gideon was glad she'd made it for several reasons. For one thing, he doubted it was true, which dented her credibility considerably, which made him feel less guilty for the sweet talking he was about to do. For another, it gave him an out. He was more than willing to wine and dine Elizabeth Abbott for the sake of the project, but he wasn't going beyond that. Hopefully, he'd have the concessions he wanted by the time dessert was done.

Actually he did even better than that. Around and between sexy smiles, the doling out of small tidbits of personal information and the withholding of enough else to make Elizabeth immensely curious, he got her to agree that though some of her reservations had merit, the pluses of the Crosslyn Rise conversion outweighed the minuses. In a golden twist of fate—not entirely bizarre, Gideon knew, since the restaurant they were at was the only place for fine evening dining in town—two other members of the zoning commission were eating there with their wives. Unable to resist showing Gideon how influential she was, Elizabeth insisted on threading her arm through his and leading him to their table, introducing him around, then announcing that she had decided not to veto the Crosslyn Rise conversion after all. The men from the commission seemed pleased. They vigorously shook hands with Gideon and welcomed him to their town, while their wives looked on with smiles. Gideon smiled as charmingly at the wives as he did at Elizabeth. He knew it would be hard for her to renege after she'd declared her intentions before so many witnesses.

Feeling proud of himself for handling things with such aplomb, he sent a wink to a waitress whose looks tickled his fancy, as he escorted Elizabeth from the restaurant. At her front door, he graciously thanked her for the pleasure of her company.

"Will we do it again?" she asked.

"By all means. Though I feel a little guilty."

"About what?"

"Seeing you, given our business dealings. There are some who would say we have a conflict of interest."

"They won't say it to me," Elizabeth claimed. "I do what I want."

"In this town, yes. But I work all over the state. I won't have you as my guardian angel other places."

Elizabeth frowned. "Are you saying that we shouldn't see each other until you're done with all of Crosslyn Rise? But that's ridiculous! The project could take years!"

In a soft, very gentle, slightly naughty voice, he said, "That's not what I'm saying at all. I'm just suggesting we wait until my work with the zoning commission is done.''

Her frown vanished, replaced by a smug smile. "It's done. You'll have your permit by ten tomorrow morning." She tugged at his lapel. "Any more problems?"

He gave her his most lecherous grin and looked at her mouth. "None at all, ma'am. What say I call you later in the week. I'm busy this weekend, but I'm sure we'll be able to find another time when we're both free." He glanced at his watch. "Almost nine. Gotta run before I turn into a mouse." He winked. "See ya."

"So what was she like?" Johnny McCaffrey asked him the next afternoon after work.

They were at Sully's, where they went most days when Gideon was home in Worcester. Sully's was a diner when the sun shone and a bar at night, the watering spot for the local rednecks. Gideon's neck wasn't as red as some, but he'd grown up with these guys. They were his framers, his plasterers, his masons. They were his teammates—softball in the summer, basketball the rest of the year. They were also his friends.

Johnny was the closest of those and had been since they were eight and pinching apples from Drattles' orchard on the outskirts of town. Ugly as sin, Johnny had a heart of gold, which was probably why he had a terrific wife, Gideon mused. He was as loyal as loyal came, and every bit as trustworthy. That didn't mean he didn't live a little vicariously through Gideon.

"She was incredible," Gideon said now of Elizabeth, and it wasn't a compliment. "She has everything going for her—blond hair, blue eyes, nice bod, great legs—then she opens her mouth and the arrogance pours out. And dim-witted? Man, she's amazing. What woman in this day and age wouldn't have seen right through me? I mean, I wasn't subtle about wanting that permit—and wanting it before I touched her. Hell, I didn't even have to *kiss* her for it."

"Too bad."

"Nah. She didn't turn *me* on." He took a swig of his beer.

Johnny tipped his own mug and found it empty. "That type used to. You must be getting old, pal. Used to be you'd take most anything, and the more hoity-toity the better." He punctuated the statement with two raps of his mug on the bar.

Gideon drew himself straighter on his stool and said with a self-mocking grin, "That was before I got hoity-toity myself. I don't need other people's flash no more. I got my own."

"Watch out you don't start believing that," Johnny teased. "Give me another, Jinko," he told the bartender. To Gideon, he said, "I bumped into Sara Thayer today. She wanted to know how you've been. She'd love a call."

Gideon winced. "Come on, Johnny. She's a kid."

"She's twenty-one."

"I don't fool with kids."

"She doesn't look like a kid. She's got everything right where it's supposed to be. And she ain't gonna wait forever."

Sara Thayer was Johnny's wife's cousin. She'd developed a crush on Gideon at a Christmas party two years before, and Johnny, bless his soul, had been a would-be matchmaker ever since. Sara was a nice girl, Gideon thought. But she *was* far too young, and in ways beyond her age.

As though answering a call, the waitress chose that moment to come close and drape an arm around Gideon's shoulder. He slid his own around her waist and pulled her close. "Now this," he told Johnny, "is the kind of woman for me. Solid and mature. Dedicated. Appreciative." He turned to her. "What do you say, Cookie? Want to go for a ride, you and me?"

Cookie snapped her gum while she thought about it, then planted a kiss on his nose. "Not tonight, big guy. I gotta work till twelve, and you'll be sound asleep by then. Hear you landed a big new job."

"Yup."

"Hear it's on the coast."

"Yup."

"Now why'd you do that for, Gideon Lowe? Every time you sign up to build something off somewhere, we don't see you so much. How long is this one gonna take?"

"A while. But I'm commuting. I'll be around."

Cookie snorted. "You better be. If I've gotta look at this guy—" she hitched her chin toward Johnny "—sittin' here with the weight of all your other jobs on his shoulders for long, I'll go nuts."

"John can handle it," Gideon said with confidence. Johnny had been his foreman for years and had never once let him down. "You just be good to him, babe, and he'll smile. Right, John?"

"Right," Johnny said.

Cookie snapped her gum by way of punctuation, then said, "You guys hungry? I got some great hash out back. Whaddya say?"

"Not for me," Johnny said. "I'm headin' home in another five."

Gideon was heading home, too, but not to a woman waiting with dinner. He was heading toward a deskful of paperwork. The idea of putting that off for just a little longer was mighty appealing.

"Is it fresh, the hash?" he asked.

Cookie cuffed him on the head.

"I'll have some," he said. "Fast." He gave Cookie a pat on the rump and sent her off.

"So you're all set to get started up there now that the permit's through?" Johnny asked.

"Yup. We'll break ground on Monday, get the foundation poured the week after, then start framing. October can be a bitch of a month if we get rain, but I really want to get everything up and closed in before the snows come."

"Think you can?"

Gideon thought about that, thought about the complex designs of the condominium clusters and the fact that the crews he used would be commuting better than an hour each way, just like he would. He'd debated using local subs, but he really wanted his own men. He trusted his own men. They knew him, knew what he demanded, and, in turn, he knew they could produce. Of course, if the weather went bad, or they dug into ledge and had to blast, things would be delayed. But with the permit now in hand, they had a chance.

"We're sure as hell gonna try," he said.

They did just that. With Gideon supervising every move, dump trucks and trailers bearing bulldozers and backhoes moved as carefully as possible over the virgin soil of Crosslyn Rise toward the duck pond, which was the first of three areas on the property being developed. After a cluster of eight condominiums was built there, another eight would be built in the pine grove, then another eight in the meadow. The duck pond had the most charm, Gideon thought and was pleased it was being developed first. Done right, it would be a powerful selling tool. That fact was foremost in his mind as the large machines were unloaded and the work began.

Fortunately, he and Carter had paved the way by having things cited, measured and staked well before the heavy equipment arrived. Though they were both determined to remove the least number of trees, several did have to come down to make room for the housing. A separate specialty crew had already done the cutting and chipping, leaving only stumping for the bulldozers when they arrived.

Once the best of the topsoil had been scraped off the top of the land and piled to the side, the bulldozers began the actual digging. Carter came often to watch, sometimes with Jessica, though the marring of the land tore her apart. She had total faith in Carter's plans and even, thanks to Carter's conviction, in Gideon's ability to give those plans form. Still, she had lived on Crosslyn Rise all her life, as had her father before her. The duck pond was only one of the spots she found precious.

Gideon could understand her feelings for the Rise. From the first time he'd walked through the land, he'd been able to appreciate its rare beauty. Being intimately involved in the work process, though, he had enough on his mind to keep sentimentality in check.

Contrary to Jessica, the deeper the hole got, the more excited he was. There was some rock that could be removed without blasting, some that couldn't but that could be circumvented by moving the entire cluster over just a bit and making a small section of one basement a bit more shallow. But they hadn't hit water, and water was what Gideon had feared. The tests had said they wouldn't, but he'd done tests before and been wrong; a test done in one spot didn't always reveal what was in another. They'd lucked out, which meant that the foundation could be sunk as deeply as originally planned, which meant less grading later and a far more aesthetically pleasing result.

The cellar hole was completed and the forms for the foundation set up. Then, as though things were going too smoothly, just when the cement was to be poured, the rains came. They lasted only three days, but they came with such force—and on a Monday, Tuesday and Wednesday—that it wasn't until the following Monday that Gideon felt the hole had dried out enough to pour the foundation.

He mightn't have minded the layoff, since there were plenty of other things to be done on plenty of other projects that his crews were involved in, had it not been for Elizabeth Abbott's calls.

"She wants to see me," he told Gordon the following Saturday at Jessica and Carter's wedding reception. He'd cornered the banker at one end of the long living room of the mansion at Crosslyn Rise. They were sipping champagne, which Gideon rather enjoyed. He wasn't particularly enjoying his tuxedo, though. He felt slightly strangled in it, but Jessica had insisted. She wanted her wedding to be elegant, and Carter, lovesick fool that he was, had gone right along with her. When Gideon got married—*if* he ever did—he intended to wear jeans.

At the moment, though, that wasn't his primary concern; Elizabeth Abbott was. "I've already put her off two or three times, but she keeps calling. I'm telling you, the woman is either stubborn or desperate. She doesn't take a hint.''

"Maybe you have to be more blunt,'' Gordon suggested. He was pursing his lips in a way that told Gideon he found some humor in the situation.

Gideon didn't find any humor in it at all. He felt a little guilty about what he'd done, leading Elizabeth on. Granted, he'd gotten his permit, which had made the entire eight-member consortium, plus numerous on-call construction workers very happy. None of the others, though, were getting suggestive phone calls.

"Oh, I can be more blunt,'' he said. "The question is whether there's anything else she can do to slow us down from here on. She's a dangerous woman. She's already shown us that. I wouldn't want to do or say anything to jeopardize this project.''

Gordon seemed to take that part a bit more seriously. He thought about it for a minute while he watched Carter lead Jessica in a graceful waltz to the accompaniment of a string quartet. "There's not much she can do now,'' he said finally. "We have written permits for each of the different phases of this project. She could decide to rescind one or the other, but I don't think she'd dare. Not after she pulled back last time, then changed her mind. I don't think she'd want people knowing that it was Carter last time and you this time.''

"It *isn't* me,'' Gideon said quickly. "I haven't slept with her. I haven't even gone *out* with her, other than that first dinner, and that was business.''

"Apparently not completely," Gordon remarked dryly.

"It was business. The rest was all innuendo." His eyes were glued to the bride and groom, moving so smoothly with just the occasional dip and twirl. "Where in the hell did Carter learn to do that? He was born on the same side of the tracks as me. The son of a bitch must've taken lessons."

Gordon chuckled. "Must've."

Gideon followed them a bit longer. "They look happy."

"I'd agree with that."

"He's a lucky guy. She's a sweetie."

"You bet."

"She got any sisters?"

"Sorry."

Gideon sighed. "Then I guess I'll have to mosey over and see if I can't charm that redheaded cutie in the sparkly dress into swaying a little with me. I'm great at swaying." He took a long sip of his champagne. After it had gone down, he put a finger under his collar to give him a moment's free breath, set his empty glass on a passing tray, cleared his throat and was off.

The redheaded cutie in the sparkly dress turned out to be a colleague of Jessica's at Harvard. She swayed with Gideon a whole lot that night, then saw him two subsequent times. Gideon liked her. She had a spark he wouldn't have imagined a professor of Russian history to have. She also had a tendency to lecture, and when she did that, he felt as though he were seventeen again and hanging on by his bare teeth, just trying to make it through to graduation so that he could start doing, full-time, what he'd always wanted, which was to build houses.

So he let their relationship, what of it there had been, die a very natural death. Elizabeth Abbott, though, wasn't so easy to dispose of. The first time she called after the wedding, he said that he had a previously arranged date. The second time, he said he was seeing the same woman and that they were getting pretty involved. The third time, he said he just couldn't date other women until he knew what was happening with this first.

"I'm not saying we have to *date*," Elizabeth had the gall to say in a slithery purr. "You could just drop over here one evening and we could let nature take its course."

He mustered a laugh. "I don't know, Elizabeth. Nature hasn't been real kind to me lately. First we had rain, now an early frost. Maybe we shouldn't push our luck."

The purr was suddenly gone, yielding to impatience. "You know, Gideon, this whole thing is beginning to smell. Have you been leading me on all this time?"

He figured she'd catch on at some point. Fortunately, he'd thought out his answer. "No. I really enjoyed the dinner we had. You're one pretty and sexy lady. It's just that I was madly in love with Marie for years before she up and married someone else. Now she's getting a divorce. I was sure there wouldn't be anything left between us, but I was wrong. So I could agree to go out with you, or drop in at your place some night, but that wouldn't be fair to you. You deserve more than a man with half a heart." *Half a heart*. Not bad, bucko.

Elizabeth wasn't at all impressed. "If she's married and divorced, she's a loser. Weak women make weak marriages. You're looking for trouble, Gideon."

"Maybe," he said, leaving allowance for that should the day come when Elizabeth found out there wasn't anyone special in his life after all, "but I have to see it through. If not, I'll be haunted forever. I have to know, once and for all, whether she and I have a chance."

She accepted his decision, though only temporarily. She continued to call every few nights to check on the status of his romance with Marie. Gideon wasn't naturally a liar and certainly didn't enjoy doing it over and over again, but Elizabeth pushed him into a corner. There were times when he thought he was taking the wrong tactic, when he half wanted to take her up on her invitation, show up at her house, then proceed to be the worst lover in the world. But he couldn't do it. He couldn't demean her—or himself—that way.

So she continued to call, and he continued to lie, all the while cursing himself for doing it, cursing Carter and Gordon for setting him up, cursing Elizabeth for being so goddamned persistent. He was fit to be tied, wondering where it would end, when suddenly, one day, at the very worst possible moment, she appeared at the site.

At least he thought it was her. The hair was blond, the clothes conservative, the figure shapely, the legs long. But it had rained the night before, and the air was heavy with mist, reducing most everything to blandly generic forms.

He was standing on the platform that would be the second floor of one of the houses in the cluster and had been hammering right along with his crew, getting an end piece ready to raise. The work was done. The men had positioned themselves. They were slowly hoisting the large, heavy piece when the creamy figure emerged from the mist.

"Jeez, what's that?" one of the men breathed, diverting the attention of a buddy. That diversion, fractional though it was, was enough to upset the alignment of the skeletal piece. It wobbled and swayed as they tried to right it.

"Easy," Gideon shouted, every muscle straining as he struggled to steady the wood. "Ea-sy." But the balance was lost, and, in the next instant, the piece toppled over the side of the house to the ground.

Gideon swore loudly, then did it again to be heard above the ducks on the pond. He made a quick check to assure himself that none of his men had gone over with the frame. He stalked to the edge of the platform and glared at the splintered piece. Then he raised his eyes and focused on the woman responsible.

2

She was dressed all in beige, but Gideon saw red. Whirling around, he stormed to the rough stairway, clattered down to the first floor, half walked, half ran out of the house and, amid fast-scattering ducks, around to where she stood. Elizabeth Abbott had been a pain in the butt for weeks, but she hadn't disturbed his work until now. He intended to make sure she didn't do it again.

The only thing was that when he came face-to-face with her, he saw that it wasn't Elizabeth. At first glance, though, it could have been her twin, the coloring was so similar. His anger was easily transferred. The fact was that *regardless* of who she was, she was standing where she didn't belong.

"What in the hell do you think you're doing, just popping up out of thin air like that?" he bellowed with his hands on his hips and fury in his voice. Disturbed by his tone, the ducks around the pond quacked louder. "In case you didn't see the sign out front, this is private property. That means that people don't just go wandering around—" he tossed an angry hand back toward the ruined framework "—and for good reason. Look what you've done. My men spent the better half of a day working on that piece, and it'll have to be done over now, which isn't real great, since we were racing to get it up before the rain started again this afternoon. And that's totally aside from the fact that someone could have been hurt in this little fiasco. I carry insurance, lady, but I don't count on people tempting fate. You could have been killed. *I* could have been killed. Any of my *men* could have been killed. A whole goddamned feast worth of *ducks* could have been killed. This is no place for tourists!''

It wasn't that he ran out of breath. He could have ranted on for a while, venting everything negative that he was feeling, only something stopped him, something to do with the woman herself and the way she looked.

Yes, her coloring was like Elizabeth's. She had fair skin, blue eyes, and blond hair that was pulled back into a neat knot. And to some extent, she was dressed as he imagined Elizabeth might have been, though he'd only seen her that one time, when she'd been wearing a dress. This woman was wearing a long pleated skirt of the same cream color as her scarf, which was knotted around the neck of a jacket that looked an awful lot like his old baseball jacket, but of a softer, finer fabric. The jacket was taupe, as were her boots. She wore large button earrings that could have been either ivory or plastic—he wasn't a good judge of things like that in the best of times, and this wasn't the best of times. He was still deeply shaken from what had happened. The look on her face, the way her eyes were wide and her hands were tucked tightly into her pockets, said that she was shaken, too.

"I'm not a tourist," she said quietly. "I know the owner of Crosslyn Rise."

"Well, if you were hoping to find her out here in the rain, you won't. She's working. If you were really a friend of hers, you'd know that."

"I know it. But I didn't come to see Jessica. I came to see what was happening here. She said I could. She was the one who suggested I do it."

If there was one thing Gideon hated, it was people who managed to hold it together when he was feeling strewn. This woman was doing just that, which didn't endear her to him in the least. "Well, she should have let me know first," he barked. "I'm the one in charge here, I ought to know what's going on. If we're having visitors to the site, I can alert my men. There's no reason why they should be shocked the way they were."

"You're right," she agreed. "What's wrong with them? Haven't they ever seen a woman before?"

She was totally innocent, totally direct and quite cutting with that last statement. Gideon shifted her closer in ilk to Elizabeth again. "Oh, they've seen women. They've seen lots of them, and in great and frequent intimacy, I'd wager. But what you just did was like a woman showing up in the men's john."

She had the gall to laugh, but it, too, had an innocent ring. "Cute analogy, though it's not quite appropriate. The sign out front says Private Way. It doesn't say No Women Allowed. Is it my fault if your men get so rattled by the sight of a woman that they become unglued? Face it. You should be yelling at them, not me.''

She had a point, he supposed, but he wasn't about to admit it. She had a quiet confidence to her that didn't need stroking. ''The fact is that your appearance here has messed us up.''

''I'm sorry for that.''

''Fine for you to be sorry, after the fact.''

''It's better than nothing, which is what I'm getting from you. You could try an apology, too.''

''For what?''

''Nearly killing me. If I'd been a little closer, or that piece had shattered and bounced, I'd be lying on the ground bleeding right now.''

He gave her a once-over, then drawled, ''That wouldn't do much for your outfit.''

''It wouldn't do much for your future, unless you have a fondness for lawsuits.''

''You don't have the basis for any lawsuit.''

''I don't know about that. You and your men were clearly negligent in this case.''

Gideon drew himself straighter, making the most of his six-foot-four-inch frame. ''So you're judge and jury rolled into one?''

She drew herself straighter to match, though she didn't have more than five foot seven to work with.

"Actually, I'm an interior designer. It may well be that I'll be working on this project."

"Not if I can help it," he said, because she was a little too sure of herself, he thought.

"Well, then," she turned to leave, "it's a good thing you're not anyone who counts. If I take this job, I'll be answerable to the Crosslyn Rise consortium, not to some job foreman who can't control his men." With a final direct look, she started off.

Gideon almost let her go. After all, they were far enough from the building that his men hadn't heard what she'd said, so he didn't have to think about saving face, at least, not before them. There was, of course, the matter of his own pride. For years he'd been fighting for respect, and he was doing it now, on several levels, with this project. The final barrier to fall would be with people like this one, who were educated and cultured and arrogant enough to choke a horse.

"You really think you're something, don't you?" he called.

She stopped but didn't turn. "No. Not really. I'm just stating the facts."

"You don't know the facts."

"I know that the consortium controls this project. It isn't some sort of workmen's cooperative."

"In some ways it is. Carter Malloy is in the consortium, and he's the architect of record. Nina Stone is in the consortium, and she'll be marketing us."

There was an expectancy to her quiet. "So?"

He savored the impending satisfaction. "So I'm not just 'some job foreman.' I'm the general contractor here. I also happen to be a member of that consortium."

For another minute, she didn't move. Then, very slowly she turned her head and looked at him, in a new light, he thought.

He touched a finger to the nonexistent visor of the wool cap perched on the top of his head. "Name's Gideon Lowe. See y'in the boardroom." With that, he turned back to his men, yelled, "Let's get this mess cleaned up," and set about doing just that with a definitive spring to his step.

Christine Gillette was appalled. She hadn't imagined that the man who'd blasted her so unfairly was a member of the consortium. Granted, he was better spoken than some of the laborers she'd met. But he'd been bullheaded and rough-hewn, not at all in keeping with the image she had of polished men sitting around a boardroom table with Jessica Crosslyn Malloy at its head.

Unsure as to what to say or do, she turned and left when he returned to his work. During the forty-minute drive back to her Belmont office, she replayed their conversation over and over in her mind and never failed to feel badly at its end. She wasn't normally the kind to cut down other people with words, though she did feel she'd had provocation. She also felt that she was right. She *had* apologized. What more could she do?

The fact remained, though, that in several weeks' time she'd be making a presentation to the Crosslyn Rise consortium. Gideon Lowe would be there, no doubt wearing a smug smile on his handsome face. She was sure he'd be the first to vote against her. Smug, handsome, physical men were like that, she knew. They defined the world in macho terms and were perfectly capable of acting on that principle alone. No way would he willingly allow her to work on his project.

She wished she could say that she didn't care, that Crosslyn Rise was just another project, that something else as good would come along. But Crosslyn Rise was special, not only in terms of the project itself but what it would mean to her. She'd been a designer for nearly ten years, working her way up from the most modest jobs—even freebies, at first—to jobs that were larger and more prestigious. This job, if she got it, would be the largest and most prestigious yet. From a designer's standpoint, given the possibilities between the condominium clusters and the mansion, it was exciting. In terms of her career, it was even more so.

Her mind was filled with these thoughts and others when she arrived at her office. Margie Dow, her secretary, greeted her with a wave, then an ominous, "Sybil Thompson's on the warpath. She's called three times in the last two hours. She says she *needs* to talk with you."

Chris rolled her eyes, took the other pink slips that Margie handed her and headed into her office. Knowing that waiting wouldn't make things any better, she dialed Sybil's number. "Hi, Sybil. It's Chris. I just this minute got back to the office. Margie tells me you have a problem."

"*I* have a problem?" Sybil asked, giving Chris a premonition of what was coming. "*You* have a problem. I just came from Stanley's. Your people put down the wrong rug."

Stanley was Sybil's husband and a lawyer, and the carpeting in question was for his new suite of offices. Chris had been hired as the decorator one short month before and had been quite blunt, when Stanley and his partners had said that they wanted the place looking great within the week, about saying that quality outfittings were hard to find off the rack. They'd agreed to the month, and she'd done her best, running back and forth with pictures and swatches and samples, placing rush orders on some items, calling around to locate others in less well-traveled outlets. Now Sybil was saying that one of those items wasn't right.

Propping a shoulder to the phone to hold it at her ear, Chris went around her desk to the file cabinet, opened it and thumbed through. "I was there yesterday afternoon when it was installed, Sybil. It's the one we ordered."

"But it's too dark. Every tiny little bit of lint shows. It'll look filthy all the time."

"No. It's elegant." She extracted a file. It held order forms, sales receipts and invoices relating to the Thompsons' account. "It goes perfectly with the rest of the decor." She began flipping through.

"It's too dark. It really is. I'm sure we chose something lighter. Check the order form and you'll see."

"That's what I'm doing right now. According to this," Chris studied the slip, "we ordered Bold Burgundy, and Bold Burgundy is the color we installed yesterday."

"It can't be."

"It is." She spoke gently, easily understanding Sybil's confusion. "Everything was done quickly. You looked at samples of carpeting, chose what you wanted, and I ordered it. When things move fast like that, with as much done at one time as you did, it's only natural to remember some things one way and some things another way. I'd do it myself, if I didn't write everything down." Of course, that wasn't the only reason she wrote everything down. The major reason was to protect herself from clients who ordered one thing, saw it installed, then decided that it wasn't what they wanted after all. She didn't know whether Sybil fell into that category or whether this was an innocent mix-up. But Chris did have the papers to back up her case.

"I suppose you're right," Sybil said. "Still, that carpet's going to look awful."

"It won't. The cleaning people come through to vacuum every night. Besides, you don't get half the lint in a lawyer's office as you get at home, especially when you're dealing with the upscale clientele that your husband is. Trust me. Bold Burgundy looks great."

Sybil was weakening. "You think so?"

"I know so. Just wait. Give it a few weeks and see what the clients say. They'll rave about it. I'm sure. That carpeting gives a rich look. They'll feel privileged to be there, without knowing why."

Sybil agreed to wait. Satisfied, Chris hung up the phone and returned the folder to the cabinet. Then she opened another drawer, removed a thick cardboard tube, slid out the blueprints for Crosslyn Rise and spread them on her desk.

Carter was brilliant. She had to hand it to him. What he'd done—taking the Georgian colonial theme from the mansion, modifying columns and balconies, elongating the roof and adding skylights to give just a hint of something more contemporary—was perfect. The housing clusters were subtle and elegant, nestling into the setting as though they'd been there forever.

She sighed. She wanted to work on this project in one regard that had nothing to do with either challenge, prestige or money. It had to do with Crosslyn Rise itself. She thought it was gorgeous, real dream material. If ever she pictured a place she would have liked to call home, it was the mansion on the rise. Doing the decorating for it was the next best thing to living there.

She wanted that job.

Picking up the phone, she dialed Jessica Malloy's Harvard office. Despite what she'd told Gideon, Jessica and she were less friends than acquaintances. They had a mutual friend, who was actually the one to suggest to Jessica that Chris do the work on the Rise. They had met after that and hit it off. Though Chris knew that other designers were being considered for the job, she was sure she could compete—unless Gideon Lowe blackballed her.

"Hi," she said to the secretary who answered, "this is Christine Gillette. I'm looking for Jessica. Has she come back from her honeymoon?"

"She certainly has," the woman said. "Hold on, please."

Less than a minute later, Jessica came on the phone. "Christine, how are you?"

"I'm fine, but, hey, congratulations on your marriage." Last time they'd talked, Jessica had been up to her ears in plans. Apparently the wedding had been something of a last-minute affair thanks to Carter, who had refused to wait once Jessica had finally agreed to marry him. "I take it everything went well?"

"Perfectly," Jessica said.

Chris could hear her smile and was envious. "And the trip to Paris?"

"Too short, but sweet."

And terribly romantic, Chris was sure. Paris was that way, or so she was told. She'd never been there herself. "I'm sure you'll get back some day. Maybe for your fiftieth anniversary?"

"Lord, we'll be doddering by then," Jessica said, laughing, and again Chris was envious. To have someone special, like Jessica had Carter, was precious. So was growing old with that someone special. She hoped Jessica knew how lucky she was.

"I wouldn't worry about doddering. You have years of happiness ahead. I wish you both all the best."

"Thanks, Chris. But enough about me. Tell me what's doing with you. You are getting a presentation ready for us, aren't you?"

"Definitely," Chris said and took a breath, "but I had a small problem this morning. I'm afraid I went out to the Rise to walk around, and I upset some of the men working there."

"You upset them? I'd have thought it'd be the other way around. What they're doing to my gorgeous land upsets me to no end."

"But the mess is only temporary. You know that."

"I know, and I'm really excited about Carter's plans and about what the Rise will be, and I know this was my only out, since I couldn't afford the upkeep, not to mention repairs and renovations—" She caught her breath. "Still, I have such sentimental feelings for the place that it's hard for me when even the smallest tree is felled."

"I can understand that," Chris said with a smile. She really liked Jessica, among other things for the fact that she wasn't a money grubber. In that sense, Chris identified with her. Yes, the conversion of Crosslyn Rise would be profitable, but it was a means to an end, the end being the preservation of the Rise, rather than the enhancement of Jessica's bank account. Likewise, Chris sought lucrative jobs like decorating Stanley Thompson's law firm, redecorating the Howard family compound on the Vineyard, and yes, doing Crosslyn Rise, for a greater cause than her own. Her personal needs were modest and had always been so.

"Tell me what happened to you, though," Jessica was saying, returning to the events of that morning.

Chris told her about appearing at the site and jinxing Gideon's crew. "It was an innocent mistake, Jessica. Honestly. I never dreamed I'd disturb them, or I never would have gone. I thought I was being unobtrusive. I just stood there, watching without saying a word, but one of the guys saw me and two others looked and then the damage was done. I really am sorry. I tried to tell your contractor that, but I'm not sure I got through."

"To Gideon? I'm sure you did. He's a sensible guy."

"Maybe when he's cool, but he was pretty hot under the collar when that framework fell, and I don't blame him. Someone could have been hurt, and then there's the time lost in having to redo the piece, and the rain that he was trying to beat. I, uh, think we may have gotten off on the wrong foot, Gideon and I. He was annoyed and said some things that irked me, so I said some irksome things back, and I may have sounded arrogant. I'm not usually like that."

"And now you're worried that he'll stand in the way of your getting this job."

"That, and that if I do get the job, he and I will have trouble working together. He's a macho type. I don't do well with macho types. I kind of pull in and get intimidated, so I guess I put up a wall, and then I come off sounding snotty. I'm sure that's what he thinks."

"He'll change his mind when he meets you in a more controlled setting."

"When there are other people, *civilized* people around, sure. But if we work together, it won't always be in that kind of controlled setting. There won't always be other people around. We'll be spending a lot of time at the site. His subs and their crews may be around, but if today was any indication, they won't be much help."

The telephone line was quiet for a minute before Jessica asked, "Are you saying that you don't want to try for the job?"

"Oh, no!" Chris cried. "Not at all! I *want* the job. I want it a *lot*!"

Jessica sounded genuinely relieved. "That's good, because I really like what I've seen of your work. It has a sensitivity that I haven't found in some of the others' things. I don't want the Rise to look done up, or glossy. I don't want a 'decorated' look. I want something different and special, something with feeling. Your work has that. *You* have that, I think."

"I hope so, at least as far as my work goes," and she was deeply gratified to hear Jessica say it. But that wasn't why she'd called. "As far as this business with Gideon Lowe goes—"

"Don't think twice about it, Chris. You may not believe it, but Gideon is really a pretty easygoing kind of guy."

"You're right. I don't believe it."

Jessica laughed. "He is. Really. But he takes his work very seriously. He may have overreacted this morning, in which case he's probably feeling like a heel, but he'll get over it. This project means a lot to him. He has money invested in it. He'd be the first one to say that when we pick people to do the work, we have to pick the best."

"Is that why he picked himself as the builder?" Chris couldn't resist tossing out. She barely had to close her eyes to picture his smug smile or the broad set of his shoulders or the tight-hipped way he'd walked away from her.

"He's good. I've seen his things. Carter has worked with him before, and *he* says he's good. Gideon's reputation's at stake here, along with his money. He wants the best. And if the best turns out to be you, once we hear all the presentations, he'll go along with it."

"Graciously?" Somehow Chris couldn't see it.

"Graciously. He's a professional."

Chris thought a lot about that in the days following. She figured Jessica might be right. Gideon was a professional. But a professional what? A professional builder? A professional businessman? A professional bruiser? A professional lover? No doubt he had a wife stashed away somewhere, waiting with the television warmed and the beer chilled for the time when he got home from work and collapsed into his vinyl recliner. Chris could picture it. He looked like that type. Large, brawny, physical, he'd be the king of whatever castle he stormed.

Then again, he was a member of the consortium. Somehow that didn't jibe with the image. To be a member of a consortium, one needed money and brains. Chris knew there was good money in building, at least for the savvy builder, and the savvy builder had to be bright. But there were brains, and there were brains. Some were limited to one narrow field, while others were broader. She didn't picture Gideon Lowe being broad in any respect but his shoulders.

That was one of the reasons why she grew more nervous as the day of the presentation drew near. She burned the midnight oil doing drawings, then redoing them, trying to get them just right. She sat back and rethought her concept, then altered the drawings yet again to accommodate even the slightest shift. She knew that, given Gideon's predisposition, she'd have to impress the others in the group in a big way if she wanted the job.

The day of the meeting was a beautiful one, cool and clear as the best of November days were along the North Atlantic shore. Gideon felt good. The first roof section had gone up despite a last-minute glitch that had kept Carter and him sweating over the plans the weekend before. But things had finally fit, and if all went well, the second, third and fourth roof sections would be up by the end of the week. Once that was done, the snows could come and Gideon wouldn't give a hoot.

It had also been eight whole days since he'd last heard from Elizabeth Abbott.

So he was in a plucky mood when the eight members of the consortium held their weekly meeting at seven that evening in Gordon's office. It occurred to Gideon as he greeted the others and took his place at the table, that he was comfortable with the group. It hadn't been so at first. He had felt self-conscious, almost like an imposter, as though he didn't have any business being there and they all knew it. Over the weeks that they'd been meeting, though, he'd found himself accepted as a peer. More than that, his status as the general contractor actually gave him a boost in their eyes. He was the one member of the group most closely aligned with the reality of the project.

There were Carter and Jessica, sitting side by side, then the three men Gordon had brought in from other areas—Bill Nolan, from the Nolan Paper Mill family in Maine, Ben Heavey, a real estate developer well-known in the East, and Zach Gould, a retired banker with time and money on his hands, who visited the site often. Rounding out the group were John Sawyer, a local bookseller, and Nina Stone, the realtor who would one day market the project.

Being single, Gideon had taken notice of Nina at the start. They'd even gone out to dinner once, but neither had wanted a follow-up, certainly not as a prelude to something deeper. Nina was a tough cookie, an aggressive woman, almost driven. Petite and a little bizarre, she wasn't Gideon's type at all. By mutual agreement, they were simply friends.

After calling the meeting to order, Gordon, who always sat in as an advisor of sorts, gave them a rundown of the money situation, then handed the meeting over to Carter, who called in, one by one, the interior designers vying for the project.

The first was a woman who worked out of Boston and had done several of the more notable condo projects there in recent years. Gideon thought her plans were pretentious.

The second was a man who talked a blue streak about glass and marble and monotonic values. Gideon thought everything about him sounded sterile.

The third was Christine Gillette, and Gideon didn't take his eyes off her once. She was wearing beige again, a suit this time, with a tweedy blazer over a solid-colored blouse and skirt, and he had to admit that she looked elegant. She also looked slightly nervous, if the faint shimmer of her silk blouse was any indication of the thudding of her heart. But she was composed, and obviously well rehearsed. She made her presentation, exchanging one drawing for another with slender fingers as she talked about recreating the ambience that she believed made Crosslyn Rise special. Her voice was soft, but it held conviction. She clearly believed in what she was saying.

Quite against his wishes, Gideon was impressed. Her eyes had glanced across his from time to time, but if she was remembering their last encounter, she didn't let on. She was cool, but in a positive way. Not haughty, but self-assured. She didn't remind him at all of Elizabeth Abbott.

At the end of her presentation she left, sent home, as the others had been, with word that a decision would be made within the week. It was obvious, though, where the group's sentiment lay.

"Christine's plans were the warmest," John Sawyer said. "I like the feeling she captured."

Zach Gould agreed. "I liked her, too. She wasn't heavy-handed like the first, or slick like the second."

"Her estimates are high," Ben Heavey reminded them. He was the most conservative of the group.

"All three are high," Nina said, "but the fact is that if we want this done right, we'll have to shell out. I have a feeling that Christine, more than the others, will be able to get us the most for the least. She seems the most inventive, the least programmed."

"I want to know what Gideon thinks," Carter said, looking straight at him. "He'll be spending more time with the decorator than the rest of us. There are things like moldings, doors, flooring and deck work that I specified in my plans but that are fully changeable if something else fits better with the decor. So, Gideon, what are your thoughts?"

Gideon, who had been slouched with an elbow on the arm of his chair and his chin on his fist, wasn't sure *what* those thoughts were. Christine was the best of the three, without a doubt, but he wasn't sure he wanted to work with her. There was something about her that unsettled him, though he couldn't put his finger on what it was.

"She's the least experienced of the lot," he finally said, lowering the fist and sitting straighter. "What's the setup of her firm?"

Jessica answered. "She's something of a single practitioner. Her office is small. She has one full-time secretary and two part-time assistants, both with degrees in decorating, both with small children. They're job-sharing. It works out well for them, and from what she says, it works out well for Chris."

"Job-sharing," John mused with a grin. "I like that." They all knew that he was a single parent, and that though he owned his bookstore, he only manned the cash register during those hours when he had a sitter for his son. He had a woman who sold books for him the rest of the time, so he was basically job-sharing, himself.

Job-sharing didn't mean a whole lot to Gideon. Men did the work in his field, and even if their bosses allowed it, which they didn't, they weren't the types to leave at one in the afternoon to take a toddler to gym-and-swim.

He wondered what the story was on Christine Gillette. The résumé she'd handed out said nothing whatsoever about her personal life. He hadn't seen a wedding band, though that didn't mean anything in this day and age. He wondered whether she had a husband at home, and was vaguely annoyed at the thought.

"Does *she* have little kids who she'll have to miss work for each time they get a cold?" he asked, looking slightly miffed.

"Whoa," said John. "Be compassionate, my friend."

But Gideon wasn't a father, and as for compassion, there seemed to be plenty in the room for Christine Gillette without his. "Carter's right. If we decide to use this woman, I'm the one who'll be working most closely with her. Job-sharing may be well and good in certain areas, but construction isn't one. If I have to order bathroom fixtures, and she's off taking the kid to Disney World over school vacation so she can't meet with me, we'll be held back." He thought the argument was completely valid and he was justified to raise it. Christine might be able to charm the pants off this consortium, but if she couldn't come through when *he* needed her, he didn't want her at all! "I keep things moving. That's the way I work. I need people who'll be there."

"Chris will be there," Jessica assured him. "There are no little ones at home. From what I've been told— and from more than one source—she puts in fifty-hour weeks."

"Still," he cautioned, "if she's a single practitioner—"

"With a secretary and assistants," Jessica put in.

"Okay, with a secretary and assistants, but she's the main mover. Both of the other candidates for this position have partners, full partners, people who could take over if something happened."

"What could happen?" Jessica asked. "Chris is in good health. She has a reputation for finishing jobs on time, if not ahead. She's efficient and effective. And she needs this job." She held up a hand before he could comment on that. "I know, I know. You're going to ask me why she's so desperate, and she's not. Not desperate. But this job could give her career a boost, and she wants that. She deserves it."

Gideon didn't want to think that Christine, with her fair-haired freshness, her poise, and legs long enough to drive a man wild, deserved a thing. "Hey, this isn't a charity. We're not in the business of on-the-job training."

"Gideon," Jessica said with a mocking scowl, "I know that. More than *anyone* here, I know it. I've lived on Crosslyn Rise all my life. I'm the one who's being torn apart that I can't leave it the way it always was—'' She stopped for a minute when Carter put a hand on her arm. She nodded, took a calming breath. ''I want the Rise to be the best it can possibly be, and if Chris wasn't the best, I wouldn't be recommending her.''

''She's a friend,'' Gideon accused, recalling what Chris had told him.

''She's a friend of a friend, but I have no personal interest in her getting this job. If anything, I was wary when my friend mentioned her to me, because I'm *not* in the business of doing favors. Then I looked at pictures of other jobs Chris has done. Now, looking at what she's come up with for us, I'm more convinced than ever that she's the right one.'' She stopped, had another thought, went on. ''Besides, there's a definite advantage to working with someone with a smaller client list. It's the old issue of being a small fish in a big pond, or vice versa. Personally, I'd rather be the big fish in Chris's pond, than a small fish in someone else's, particularly since no one else's ideas for this project are anywhere near as good as hers.''

Gideon might have said more, but didn't. Clearly the others agreed with Jessica, as the vote they took several minutes later proved. Christine was approved as the decorator for Crosslyn Rise by a unanimous vote. Or a nearly unanimous one. Gideon abstained.

"Why did you do that?" Carter asked quietly after the meeting had adjourned and most of the others had left.

Gideon didn't have a ready answer. "I don't know. Maybe because she didn't need my vote. She had the rest of you wowed."

"But you like her ideas."

"Yes, I like her ideas."

"Think you can work with her?"

Gideon jammed his fists into his pockets and rocked back on his heels. "Work with her? I suppose."

"So what bothers you?"

"I don't know."

Carter was beginning to have his suspicions, if the look on Gideon's face went for anything. "She's pretty, and she's single."

"Single?" Somehow that made Gideon feel worse.

"Single. Available. Is that a threat?"

"Only if she's on the make. Is she looking for it?"

"Not that I know of." Carter leaned closer. "Word has it she lives like a monk."

Gideon glowered. "Is that supposed to impress me?"

"If you're worried about being attacked, it should."

"Attacked? Me? By *her*? That's the last thing I'm worried about. Listen, man, I've got plenty of women to call when I get the urge. Snap my fingers, there they are."

"Christine isn't likely to do that."

"Don't you know it. She's the kind to snap *her* fingers. Well, I don't come running so fast, and I don't give a damn *how* pretty she is. Long legs are a dime a dozen. So are breasts, bottoms and big blue eyes, and as far as that blond hair of hers goes, it's probably right out of a bottle." He paused only for the quickest breath. "I can work with her. As long as she produces, I can work with her. But if she starts playing games, acting high and mighty and superior, and botching things up so *my* work starts looking shabby, we'll be in trouble. Big trouble."

Actually Gideon was in big trouble already, but it wasn't until three weeks had passed, during which time he couldn't get Christine Gillette out of his mind for more than a few hours at a stretch, that he realized it. The realization was driven home when she called to make an appointment to see him and he hung up the phone with a pounding heart and a racing pulse.

3

Christine was having a few small physical problems of her own as she left Belmont early that Thursday morning and headed north toward Crosslyn Rise. Her stomach was jumpy. Tea hadn't helped. Nor had a dish of oatmeal. Worse, the jitters seemed to echo through her body, leaving a fine tremor in her hands.

It was excitement, she told herself. She'd been flying high since receiving the call from Jessica that she'd landed the Crosslyn Rise job. She'd also been working her tail off since then to get ahead on other projects so that she'd have plenty of time to devote to the Rise. So maybe, she speculated as she turned onto Route 128, the trembling was from fatigue.

Then again, maybe it was nervousness. She didn't like to think so, because she'd never felt nervous this way about her work, but she'd never worked with anyone like Gideon Lowe before. She'd always managed to keep her cool, at least outwardly, with even the most intimidating of clients, but Gideon was something else. He was large, though she'd worked with larger men. He was quick-tempered, though she'd worked with some even more so. He was chauvinistic, though heaven knows she'd met worse. But he got to her as the others hadn't. He stuck in her mind. She wasn't quite sure why.

As the car cruised northward on the highway, she pondered that, just as she had been doing practically every free minute since her interview at the bank three weeks before.

She'd been slightly stunned to see him there—not to see him, per se, but to see how he looked. At the site, he'd been a craftsman. His work boots had been crusted with dirt, his jeans faded and worn. He'd been wearing a down vest, open over a plaid flannel shirt, which was open over a gray T-shirt dotted with sweat in spite of the cold. His dark hair had stuck out in a mess around the wool cap he wore. He needed a shower and a shave.

When she saw him at the bank, he'd had both. His hair was neatly combed, still longer than that of the other men in the room, though cut well. His jaw was smooth and tanned. His shoulders looked every bit as broad under a camel hair blazer as under a down vest. He knew how to knot a tie, even how to pick one, if indeed he'd picked out the paisley one he wore. And in the quick look she'd had, when the men had briefly stood as she entered then left the room, his gray slacks had fit his lean hips nearly as nicely as had a pair of jeans.

He was an extremely good-looking man, she had to admit, though she refused to believe that had any-thing to do with her nervousness. After all, she'd already decided that he was married, and anyway, she wasn't on the lookout for a man. She had one, a very nice one named Anthony Haskell, who was even-tempered and kind and took her to a show or a movie or to dinner whenever she had the time, which wasn't often. She didn't see him more than two or three times a month. But he was pleasant. He was an amiable escort. That was all she asked, all she wanted from a man—light companionship from time to time as a break from the rest of her life.

So, Gideon Lowe wasn't any sort of threat to her in that regard. Still he was so *physical*. A woman couldn't be within arm's reach of him and not feel his force. Hell, she'd been farther away than that in the boardroom at the bank, and she'd felt it. It started with his eyes and was powerful.

So he was slightly intimidating, she admitted with a sigh, and that was why she was feeling shaky. Of course, she couldn't let him know that. She'd taken the bull by the horns and called him for an appointment, making sure to sound fully composed, for that reason. Gideon looked to be the predatory type. If he sensed weakness, he'd zoom right in for the kill.

Fortifying herself with the determination to do the very best job for Crosslyn Rise that she possibly could, she turned off the highway and followed the shore road. Actually she would have preferred meeting Gideon at the bank or at Carter's office, either of which were safer places, given what had happened on that last misty morning. But Gideon had said that they should see what they were discussing, and she supposed he had a point.

The good news was that the day was sunny and bright, not at all like that other misty one. The bad news was that it was well below freezing, as was perfectly normal for December. There had already been snow, though barely enough to shovel. She couldn't help but wonder how Gideon's men kept from freezing as they worked.

As for her, she'd dressed for the occasion. She was wearing wool tights under wool slacks, a heavy cowlneck sweater and a long wool coat. Beside her on the seat were a pair of mittens and some earmuffs. It had occurred to her that Gideon was testing her mettle, deliberately subjecting her to adverse conditions, but if so, she wasn't going to come up short. She could handle subfreezing weather. She'd done it many times before.

Of course, that didn't mean that she was thrilled to be riding in her car dressed as heavily as she was. If it hadn't been for the seat belt, she'd have shrugged out of her coat. She'd long since turned down the heat, and even then, by the time she arrived at Crosslyn Rise, she felt a trickle of perspiration between her breasts.

She drove directly to the duck pond over the trail that the trucks had made, but when she reached it, it looked deserted. There wasn't a car or truck in sight. She sat for a minute, then glanced at her watch. They'd agreed on eight-thirty, which it was on the nose. Gideon had told her, a bit arrogantly, she thought, that his men started work an hour before that. But she didn't see a soul working on this cold, crisp morning. She opened her door and stepped out. The only noise came from the ducks, their soft, random quacks a far cry from the sharp sounds of construction.

Slipping back into the car, she turned it around and retraced the trail to the point where the main driveway led to the mansion. She followed it, parked and went up the brick walk, under the ivy-draped portico, to the door. Putting her face to the sidelight, she peered inside.

The place was empty. Jessica and Carter had finally finished clearing things out, putting some in storage, selling others in a huge estate sale held several weekends before. The idea was for Gideon's men to spend the worst of the winter months inside, working on the renovations that would eventually make the mansion into a central clubhouse, health center and restaurant for the condominium complex. Whether Jessica and Carter would buy one of the condo units was still undecided. For the time being, they were living in Carter's place in Boston.

Reaching into her pocket, Chris took out the key Jessica had given her and let herself into the mansion. Seconds later, she was standing in the middle of the rotundalike foyer. Ahead of her was the broad sweeping staircase that she found so breathtaking, to the right the spacious living room lit by knee-to-ceiling windows bare of drapes, to the left the similarly bright dining room.

That was the direction in which she walked, her footsteps echoing through the silent house. As she stood under the open arch, looking from window to window, chandelier to wall sconce, spot to spot where paintings had so recently hung, she imagined the long, carved mahogany table dominating the room once more. The last time it had been used was for the wedding, and though she hadn't been there, she could easily picture its surface covered with fine linen, then silver tray after silver tray of elegantly presented food. Giving herself up to a moment of fancy, she felt the excitement, heard the sounds of happiness. Then she blinked, and those happy sounds were replaced by the loud and repeated honking of a horn.

She hurried back to the front door in time to see Gideon climb from his truck. He was wearing his work clothes with nothing more than the same down vest, which surprised her, given the weather. So he was hot-blooded. She should have guessed that.

"I thought we agreed to meet down there," he said by way of greeting. He looked annoyed. "I've been waiting for ten minutes."

She checked her watch. "Not ten minutes, because I was there five minutes ago. When you didn't show, I thought I'd take a look around here. Where is everyone? It's a gorgeous day. I thought for sure there'd be work going on one place or the other."

"There will be," Gideon said, holding her gaze as he approached. Stopping a few feet away, he hooked his hands on his hips. "The men are picking up supplies. They'll be along." He smirked. "This works out really well, don't you think? We can talk about whatever it is you want to talk about, then you can be long gone by the time they get here, so they can work undisturbed."

His reference to what had happened the last time was barely veiled. The look in his eye took it a step further with the implication that she'd been the one at fault. That bothered her. "You deliberately planned it this way, I take it."

He scratched his head, which was hatless, though from the looks of his hair, he'd just tumbled out of bed, stuck on his clothes and come. The thought made her feel warmer than she already was.

"Actually," he said, "the guys had to pick up the stuff either today or tomorrow anyway. After you and I arranged to meet, today sounded real good."

"It's a shame. I was hoping they'd be here. They'll have to get used to seeing me around. I will be, more and more, once things get going."

His smirk deteriorated. "Yeah. Well . . ."

"They won't bother *me* if that's got you worried," she went on, gaining strength from her own reassuring tone. "I'm with workmen all the time. It's part of my job. Plumbers, plasterers, painters—you name it, I've seen it. They may not love having me poking around, but at least if they know I'll be wandering in from time to time, they won't be alarmed when it happens.''

"My men weren't alarmed," Gideon argued, "just distracted at a very critical time."

"Because they weren't expecting me. They had no idea who I was. Maybe it would help if I met them."

"It wouldn't help at all! You don't have any business with them. You have business with *me*!" He eyed her with sudden suspicion. "You want them around for protection, I think. You don't like being alone with me. Is that it? Is that what this is about? Because if it is—" he held both hands up "—I can assure you, you're safe. I don't fool with the hired help. And I don't fool with blondes."

"I'm relieved to hear *that*," she said, deliberately ignoring the business about "hired help" because it was a potential firecracker. The other was easier to handle. "What's wrong with blondes?"

"They're phony."

"Like rednecks are crude?"

Gideon glared at her for a minute, looking as though there were a dozen other derogatory things he wanted to say. Before he could get any out, though, she relented and said, "Look, I'm sorry. I'm not here to fight. I have a job to do, just like you. Name-calling won't help."

He continued to glare. "*Do* I make you nervous?"

"Of course not. Why would you think that?"

"You were nervous at the meeting at the bank."

And she thought she'd looked so calm. So much for show. "There were eight people—nine, counting the banker—at that meeting. I was auditioning for a job I really wanted. I had a right to be nervous." She wondered how he'd known, whether they'd all seen it or whether those dark gray eyes were just more keen than most.

"Were you surprised when you got the job?" he asked innocently enough.

"In a way. The others have bigger names than I do."

Again, innocently, he asked, "Did you think that I'd vote against you?"

"That thought did cross my mind."

"I didn't."

"Thank you."

"I abstained."

"Oh." She felt strangely hurt, then annoyed. "Well. I appreciate your telling me that. I'm glad to know you think so highly of my work."

He didn't blink. "I think your work is just fine, but I don't relish the idea of working with you. We rub each other the wrong way, you and me. I don't know why, but we do."

That about said it all. There wasn't much she could add. So she stood with her hands buried deep in the pockets of her coat, wondering what he'd say next. He seemed bent on throwing darts at her. She imagined that if she let him do it enough, let him get every little gripe off his chest, they might finally be able to work together.

Unfortunately, the darts stung.

He stared at her for a long, silent time, just stared. Holding her chin steady and her spine straight, she stared right back.

"Nothing to say?" he asked finally.

"No."

He arched a brow. "Nothing at all?"

She shook her head.

"Then why are we here?"

Chris felt a sudden rush of color to her face. "Uh, we're here to discuss business," she said, and hurried to gather her thoughts. Something had happened. Gideon's eyes must have momentarily numbed her mind. "I want to see where you're at with the condos. I thought maybe I could get a bead on things like roofing materials, stairway styles and so on." She stopped, took a deep breath, recomposed herself. "But I told you all that when I called. You were the one who said we should walk through what you've done." She gestured in the direction of the duck pond. "Can we?"

He shrugged. "Sure." He turned back toward his truck. "Climb in. I'll drive you down."

"Thanks, but I'll follow in my car."

He stopped and turned back. "Climb *in*. I'll drive you back here when we're done."

"That's not necessary," she said, but there was a challenge in his look. She wasn't sure whether it had to do with the idea of their being alone in the cab of a pickup or the idea of her climbing into a pickup, period, but in either case she had a point to make. "Okay. Let me get my purse." Crossing the driveway to her car, she took the large leather satchel in which she carried pen and paper, along with other necessities of life such as a wallet, tissues, lip gloss and appointment book. Hitching the bag to her shoulder, she grabbed her earmuffs and mittens. Then, putting on a show of confidence, she walked to the passenger's side of the truck, opened the door and climbed up.

"That was smooth," Gideon remarked.

She settled herself as comfortably as she could, given that she felt rattled. "My father is an electrician. I've been riding around in trucks all my life." And she knew how intimate they could be. A truck was like a man's office, filled with personal belongings, small doodads, tokens of that man's life. It also had his scent. Gideon's was clean, vaguely leathery, distantly coffee flavored, thanks to a half-filled cup on the console, and overwhelmingly male. She felt surrounded by it, so much so that it was a struggle to concentrate on what he was saying.

"Funny, you don't look like the type."

She swallowed. "What type?"

"To have an electrician for a father. I'd have thought your old man would be the CEO of some multinational corporation. Not an electrician."

Another dart hit home. She bristled. "There's nothing wrong with being an electrician. My father is honest and hardworking. He takes pride in what he does. *I'm* proud of what he does. And who are *you* to say something like that?''

''You asked. I answered.'' He shrugged. ''I still don't peg you as the type to be around trucks.''

''You think I'm lying?''

''No. But I think you could.''

''What's *that* supposed to mean?''

''That I'd more easily believe you if you said you've had a silver spoon in your mouth for most of your life, got bored with doing nothing, so decided to dabble around as a decorator. Real estate and interior decorating—those are the two fields women go into when they want people to think they're aggressive little workers.''

That dart hurt more than the others, no doubt because she was already bruised. ''You don't know what you're talking about,'' she said.

''If the shoe fits, wear it.''

His smug look did it. Turning to face him head-on, she said, ''Well, it doesn't. And, quite frankly, I resent your even suggesting it. I work hard, probably harder than you do, and so do most of the women I know in *either* of the fields you mentioned. We have to work twice as hard to get half the respect, thanks to people like you.'' She took a fast breath. ''And as for 'types,' I didn't have a silver spoon in my mouth at birth or at any *other* time in my life. My parents couldn't afford silver, or silk, or velvet, but they gave me lots and lots of love, which is clearly something you know nothing about. I feel badly for your wife, or your woman, whoever the hell it is you go home to at night." She reached for the door. "I'll take my own car, after all. Being cooped up in a truck with you is oppressive." In a second, she was out the door and looking back at him. "Better still, I think maybe we'd better do this another time. I'm feeling a little sick to my stomach."

Slamming the door, she stalked back to her car. She was trembling, and though she doubted he could see, she wouldn't have cared. She felt pervasive anger and incredible hurt, neither of which abated much as she sped back to Belmont. By the time she was back in her office, sitting at her desk with the door closed on the rest of the world, she was also feeling humiliated.

He'd won. He'd badgered her and she'd crumbled. She couldn't believe she'd done that. She prided herself on being strong. Lord knows, she'd had to overcome adversity to get where she was. She'd faced critics far more personal and cutting than Gideon Lowe and survived. With him, though, she'd fallen apart.

She was ashamed of herself.

She was also frightened. She wanted, *needed* to do Crosslyn Rise. By running, she may well have blown her credibility. If she'd thought working with Gideon was going to be hard before, it could well be impossible now. He'd seen her weakness. He could take advantage of it.

He could also spread word among the consortium members about what had happened, but she doubted he'd do that. He wasn't exactly an innocent party. He wouldn't want the others to know of his part. He had an image to protect, too.

Then again, he could lie. He could tell them that she made appointments, showed up, then took off minutes later. He could say that she wasted his time. He could suggest that she was mentally unbalanced.

If he spread that kind of word around, she'd be in a serious fix. Crosslyn Rise was supposed to make her career, not break it!

What to do, what to do. She sat at her desk with her feet flat on the floor, her knees pressed together, her elbows on the glass surface, her clasped hands pressed to her mouth, and wondered about that. She could call Jessica, she supposed. But she'd done that once regarding Gideon. To do it again would be tattling. Worse, it would smack of cowardice. Jessica might well begin to wonder what kind of woman she'd hired.

Nor could she call Carter. Gideon was his friend.

And she certainly couldn't call Gideon. They'd only get into another fight.

But she had to do something. She'd committed herself to Crosslyn Rise. Her reputation, her future was on the line.

The phone rang. She watched the flashing light turn solid when Margie picked it up. Distractedly she glanced at the handful of pink slips on the desk, all telephone messages waiting to be answered. She shuffled them around. Nothing interesting caught her eye.

The intercom buzzed. "Chris, you have a call from a Gideon Lowe. Do you want to take it, or should I take a message?"

Gideon Lowe. Chris's pulse skittered, then shot ahead. She didn't want to talk with him now. She was still stinging from his last shots. And embarrassed. And confused. And feeling less sure of herself than she had in years and years.

Did she want to take the phone? *No!* But that was foolish.

Bolstering herself with a deep breath, she said to Margie, "I'll take it." But she didn't pick up Gideon's call immediately. It took a few deep breaths, plus several seconds with her eyes shut tight before she felt composed enough. Even then, her finger shook when she punched in the button.

"Yes, Gideon." She wanted to sound all business. To her own ear though, she sounded frightened, just as she was feeling inside. She waited for him to blast her about driving off, leaving their meeting almost before it had begun. But he didn't say a thing. She looked at the telephone, thinking that maybe they'd been cut off. "Hello?"

"I'm sorry," he said in as quiet a tone as she'd heard from him yet. "That was not very nice of me. I shouldn't have said those things. Any of them."

"Then why did you?" she cried, only then realizing how personally she'd taken his barbs. She didn't understand *why* they bothered her so, since she and Gideon weren't anything more to each other than two people temporarily working together. But the fact was that they did, and she was upset enough to lose the cool she'd struggled to gain in the moments before she'd picked up the phone.

"Do you have something special against me?" she asked. "Have I ever done anything to you that warrants what you've been doing? I mean, I wandered innocently onto the site one day and was standing there, minding my own business, when your men saw me and botched the work they were doing. Forget that it wasn't my fault. I apologized, but it didn't make any difference. You've had it in for me ever since. Am I missing something here? Do I remind you of someone else, maybe someone unpleasant, someone who hurt you once, or who let you down? Why do you *hate* me?"

She ran out of breath. In the silence that ensued, she heard all that she'd blurted out and was appalled. She'd blown professionalism to bits, but then, that was something she seemed to do a lot in Gideon's company. She was debating hanging up the phone and burying her head in the trash can when he spoke again. His voice was still low. He actually sounded troubled.

"I don't hate you. I just look at you and... something happens. I can't explain it. Believe me, I've been trying. I've worked with lots of people over the years, lots of women, and I've never been this way before. People usually think I'm easygoing."

Chris recalled Jessica saying something to that extent. She hadn't believed it then, and she didn't believe it now. "Easygoing, like an angry bull," she murmured.

"I heard that. But it's okay. I deserve it."

In response to the confession, she softened a bit. "If you've never been this way before, then it's me. What is it I'm doing wrong? I'm trying. Really I am. I'm trying to be agreeable. I felt we should talk, because that's part of my job, and when you wanted to meet at the site, I agreed, even though it wasn't my first choice. I try to overlook some of the things you say, but they hurt, you know. I'm not a shallow person. I haven't gotten anything in life for free. I work hard at what I do, and I'm proud of that. So why do I annoy you so much?"

He was a minute in answering, and then he didn't get out more than a word when he was cut off by the operator. "All right, all right," he muttered. "Hold on Chris."

She was puzzled. "Where are you?"

She heard the clink of coins, then, "At a pay phone in town. The phones have been taken out at the Rise, and none of the ones on the street take credit cards. Can you believe that? We're building a complex that's state-of-the-art as far as living goes, in the middle of a town that's old-fashioned as hell. I'm probably gonna have to get a car phone before this project is done."

"Truck phone."

"Hmm?"

She sat back in her chair. "You drive a truck. Wouldn't you call it a truck phone?"

"I don't know. Do they? The guys who make them?"

"Beats me."

"You don't have a phone in your car?"

"No. They're expensive. Besides, I like silence when I drive. It gives me a chance to think."

"Aren't you worried about making the most of every minute?" he asked.

"I am. Making the most, that is. Thinking is important."

"Yeah, but all I hear from people is that I could be answering phone calls, communicating with clients, even getting new jobs if I had a phone in my car. Don't all those things apply to you?"

Chris had heard the arguments, too. "If someone is so desperate for my work that they can't wait until I get back into my office to talk with me, I don't want the job. You can bet it would be a nightmare. Even the most simple jobs run into snags. But one where the client wants instant satisfaction? I'll pass those up, thanks. I'm no miracle worker." She tacked on a quiet, "I wish I was."

"If you were, what would you do?"

She took another deep breath, a calmer one this time. She'd settled down, she realized. When he wasn't yelling at her, Gideon's deep voice was strangely soothing. "Wave my magic wand over you so that whatever it is that bugs you about me would disappear. I want to do a good job at Crosslyn Rise. I'm a perfectionist. But I'm also a pacifist. I can't work in an atmosphere of hostility."

"I'm not feeling hostile now."

She thought about the conversation they were having, thought about the civility that they'd somehow momentarily managed to achieve. Her heart started beating faster, in relief, she figured. "Neither am I."

"That's 'cause we're talking on the phone. We're not face-to-face."

"What is it about my *face* that bugs you, then?"

"Nothing. It's beautiful."

The unexpected compliment left Chris speechless. Before she had a chance to start stammering simply to fill in the silence, Gideon said, "You guessed right, though. That first time, I thought you were someone else. She'd been such a royal pain in the butt that I guess I took my frustration out on you." Elizabeth had called the week before; he told her he was still seeing Marie. "After that, I couldn't confuse you with her. You're different."

Chris didn't know whether that was a compliment or not. She was still basking in the first, though she felt foolish for that. What did it matter that Gideon thought she was beautiful? He was someone she'd be working with. By all rights, she should be furious that he was thinking of her in terms of looks rather than ability. He was as sexist as they came. And as deceitful, if indeed he was married.

"Uh, Chris?" He sounded hesitant.

"Yes."

"I think there's something we ought to get straight right about now. What you said before in the truck about me and a wife or a woman or whoever—"

Her heart was hammering again. "Yes?"

"There isn't any wife. I'm not married. I was once, for a real short time, years ago. But I liked having fun more than I liked being married. So it died."

Chris felt a heat in the area of her breasts that had nothing to do with her heavy cowl-neck sweater. She almost resented his saying what he'd said, though deep down she'd known he wasn't married. But they had actually been getting along. Now, having his availability open and confirmed threw a glitch into the works. "Why are you telling me this?"

"Because I think it's part of the problem. For me, at least. I'm single, and you're single. Every time I look at you I get a little bothered."

"Bothered?" If he meant what she thought he meant, they were in trouble. Suddenly she didn't want to know. "Listen, if you're worried about me, don't be. I won't accost you. I'm not in this business to pick up men."

"That's not what I meant—"

"In fact," she cut in, "I'm not looking for a man at all. There's someone I've been seeing for a while, and he's a really nice guy, but to tell you the truth, I don't even have much time for him. I spend all my free time working."

"What fun is *that*?" Gideon asked indignantly.

On the defensive again, she sat straighter. "It's plenty of fun. I enjoy my work—except for those times when I get cut to ribbons by builders who take pleasure in making other people miserable."

"I don't do it on purpose. That's what I'm trying to tell you."

"Well, try something else. Try changing. Don't assume things about me, or make value judgments. Just because I think or act differently from you, doesn't mean that I'm wrong. I don't tell you what to like. Don't tell *me* what to like."

"I'm not *doing* that," Gideon insisted. "I'm just expressing my opinion. So I express it in a way that you find offensive. Well, maybe you're too sensitive."

"Maybe I'm human! Maybe I like to get along with people. Maybe I like to please them. Maybe I like to have their respect every once in a while."

"How can you have my respect," he threw back, "if you don't hang around long enough for me to get to know you? You got upset by what I said, so instead of sticking around and fighting it out, you took off. That doesn't solve anything, Chris."

Her hand tightened on the phone. "Ah. I knew we'd get around to that sooner or later. Okay. Why don't you say what you think, just get it off your chest. I'm already feeling crushed. A little more won't hurt."

He didn't say a word.

"Go on, Gideon. Say something. I know you're dying to. Tell me that I'm a coward. Tell me that you were being overly optimistic when you abstained in that vote. Tell me that you seriously doubt whether I have the wherewithal to make it through the decorating of Crosslyn Rise." She paused, waiting. "Tell me I'm in the wrong field. Tell me I should be doing something like secretarial work. Or teaching. Or waitressing." She paused again. "Go ahead. Be my guest. I'm steeled for it." A third time, she paused. Then, cautiously she said, "Gideon?"

"Are you done?"

She was relieved that he hadn't hung up. "Yes."

"Want to meet me for lunch tomorrow?"

That wasn't what she'd expected to hear. She was taken totally off guard. "Uh, uh—"

"Maybe you were right. Maybe what we need is a neutral place to talk. So you choose it. Wherever you want to go, we'll go. I can drive down there, you can drive up here, we can meet somewhere in the middle. But we both have to eat lunch. We can even go dutch if you want. I'm perfectly willing to pay, but you women have a thing about a man treating you. Heaven forbid you might feel a little indebted to him."

"That's not why we do it. We do it because it's the professional thing to do."

"If that's so, why is it that when I go out for a business lunch with another guy, one of us usually pays, with the understanding that the other'll do it the next time? Sometimes it's easier just to charge it rather than split the bill in two. But modern women have to make things so hard."

"Then why do you bother with us?"

"I don't, usually. On my own time, I steer as far away from you as I can get. Give me the secretary or the teacher or the waitress any day. They're not hung up on proving themselves. They like it when a man opens the door for them, or helps them with their coat, or holds their chair. They like to be treated like women."

"So do I."

"Could've fooled me."

"You were the one who suggested we go dutch. If you want to pay for lunch, be my guest. You probably make a whole lot more money than I do, anyway."

"What makes you think that?" he asked.

"You've invested in Crosslyn Rise, haven't you?"

"Yeah. With every last cent I had to my name. As far as cash flow goes, I'm just about up the creek."

"Was that a wise thing to do?"

"Ask me that two years from now and I may have an answer. I've got a whole lot riding on—" The telephone clicked, cutting him off. He came back in ripe form. "Damn, I'm out of change. Look, Chris, will you meet me or not?"

"Uh, tomorrow?" She looked at her calendar. "I wouldn't be able to make it until two. My morning's wild."

The phone clicked again. "Two is fine," he said hurriedly. "Name the place."

"Joe's Grille. It's in Burlington. Right off the Middlesex Turnpike."

"Joe's Grille at two. See you then."

She wasn't sure whether he hung up the phone or the operator cut him off, but after a minute of silence, she heard a dial tone. As the seconds passed, it seemed to grow louder and more blaring, almost like an alarm, and well it might have been. She'd arranged to see Gideon again. Granted, the conditions were more to her liking this time, but still she felt uneasy.

He was a very, very confusing man, annoying her most of the time, then, in the strangest ways and when she least expected it, showing charm. Not that she was susceptible to the charm. She'd made it clear that she wasn't available, and it was true. Still, she wished he was married. She'd have felt safer that way.

But he wasn't. And the fact was that they'd be working together. It helped some to know how much Crosslyn Rise meant to him. If he was telling the truth about his financial involvement, he couldn't afford to have anything go wrong, which ruled out his sabotaging her work. And he hadn't suggested that she pull out of the project. She'd given him the chance, had all but put the words into his mouth, but he hadn't used them.

That was the up side of the situation. The downside was the lunch that she'd stupidly agreed to. A meeting at the bank would have been better. Being in a restaurant, having lunch with Gideon seemed so... personal.

But she was a professional with a job to do. So she'd meet him, and she'd be in full control, and she'd show him that she was done being bullied. She could stand up to him. It was all a matter of determination.

4

Gideon was looking forward to lunch. He felt really good after their phone conversation, as though they'd finally connected, and that mattered to him. Despite everything that he found wrong with Chris, she intrigued him. She wasn't what he'd first assumed her to be. He suspected she wasn't what, even now, he assumed her to be. She was a mystery, and he was challenged.

He was also excited in a way that had nothing to do with making progress on Crosslyn Rise and everything to do with having a date with an attractive woman. Because it was a date. Chris could call it a professional lunch, and it was, a little, but in his mind it was first and foremost a date. His motives were far from professional. He wanted to get to know Chris, wanted to start to unravel the mystery that she was. "Start" was the operative word, of course, because he envisioned this as only the first of many dates. She had already proclaimed that she wasn't looking for a man, so clearly she wasn't going to be rushed. But there'd be fun in that. Gideon was anticipating the slow, increasingly pleasant evolution of their relationship.

This first date was very important in that it would be laying the groundwork for those to come. For that reason, he was determined to be on his best, most civil and urbane behavior. He would have liked to add sophisticated or cultured to that, only he wasn't either of those things. Pretending might have worked with Elizabeth, but it wouldn't work with Chris. She'd see through him in a minute. She was sharp that way— knew damn well that he hadn't been waiting at the duck pond for ten minutes and caught him on it, though he'd only exaggerated a little. But he didn't want to be caught again, not when he wanted to impress. So he'd be himself, or that part of himself that would be most apt to please her.

For starters, he dressed for the occasion. Though he was at Crosslyn Rise at seven-thirty with the rest of his men and put in a full morning of work, he left them on their own at midday and drove all the way home to clean up. After showering and shaving, he put on a pair of gray slacks, a pink shirt, a sweater that picked up variations of those shades, and loafers. It was his yuppie outfit, the one he'd bought in Cambridge on the day he had decided to invest in Crosslyn Rise. He figured that he owed himself a small extravagance before the big splurge, and that he could use the clothes. He hated shopping. But he had to look the part of the intelligent investor, and so he'd bought the outfit, plus a blazer, two ties and a blue shirt. But he liked the pink one, at least to wear for Chris. She'd appreciate the touch.

After all, rednecks didn't wear pink.

He also put on the leather jacket that his mother had sent him several birthdays ago. It was one of the few gifts she'd given him that he liked. Most of the others were too prissy, reminding him of all she wanted him to be that he wasn't. The leather jacket, though, was perfect. It was conservative in style and of the richest brown leather he'd ever seen. He wore it a lot.

Leaving his truck in the yard, he took the Bronco, allowing plenty of time for traffic, and headed for Burlington. The route was the same to Crosslyn Rise. There were times when he felt he could do it in his sleep, except that he liked driving. Chris used her road time to think; he used his to relax, which was why he resisted getting a car phone, himself. A phone would interfere with his music. With sophisticated stereo setups in both of his vehicles, his idea of heaven was cruising along the highway at the fastest speed the traffic would bear, listening to Hank Jr., Willie or Waylon.

He didn't listen to anyone now, though, because he was too busy thinking about Chris. She really was a knockout, pretty in a soft-as-woman kind of way, despite the air of professionalism she tried to maintain. She turned him on. Oh, yeah. There was no mistaking the heat she generated. He was old enough and experienced enough—and blunt enough—to call a spade a spade. Sure, he was a little nervous to see her. Sure, it was cold outside. Sure, he hadn't eaten since six that morning. But the tiny tremors he felt inside weren't from any of those things. They were from pure, unadulterated lust.

That was the last thing he wanted Chris to know. And since it got worse the longer he thought about her—and since she was probably sharp enough to see *that* first thing, if he didn't do something to cool off— he opened the windows, turned on the music and began to sing at the top of his lungs. By the time he turned off the Middlesex Turnpike into the parking lot of Joe's Grille, his cheeks were red from the cold, his voice faintly hoarse, and his hands, as they pushed a comb through his windblown hair, slightly unsteady. He pulled on his jacket, checked the rearview mirror one last time to make sure he looked all right, took a breath and stepped out.

He was early. They were supposed to meet at two, and it was ten before the hour. He went into the restaurant just to make sure she hadn't arrived, gave his name to the hostess, along with a five for a good table and a wink for good cheer, then entered the adjoining mall and, hands stashed in his pockets, started walking around. With less than three weeks to go before Christmas, the holiday season was in full bloom. One store window was more festive, more glittery, more creative than the next. Almost as an escape from tinsel overload, he found himself gravitating toward the center of the mall, where a huge tree stood, decorated not with the usual ornaments, but with live flowers.

He stood there for a while, looking at the tree, thinking how pretty it was and that he didn't think he'd ever seen one quite like it before.

"I'm sorry," someone gasped beside him. He looked quickly down to see Chris. Her cheeks were flushed, and she was trying to catch her breath, but there was the hint of a smile on her face, even as she pressed a hand to her chest. "I got here a few minutes early, so I thought I'd pick up a gift or two, only the salesperson messed things up at the register and didn't know how to correct it, so I had to stand around waiting while he got his supervisor. The store was at the other end of the mall. I had to race back." She barely paused. "Have you been here long?"

"Not long," he said. He wondered if she was babbling because she was nervous, and hoped it was a good sign. "I was just wandering around. Everything's so pretty." But Chris took the cake. She was wearing a navy sweater and slacks and a long beige coat with a wool scarf hanging down the lapels. She might have pulled off the business look if it hadn't been for her cheeks and her hair, a few wisps of which had escaped its knot and were curling around her face, and her mouth, which looked soft, and her eyes, which were blue as the sky on a clear summer's day.

It struck him that she was more beautiful than the tree, but he wasn't about to say it. She thought she was here on business, and business partners didn't drool over each other. So he looked back at the tree. "I've never seen one decorated this way. The flowers are pretty. How do they stay so fresh?''

He hadn't actually been expecting an answer, but Chris had one nonetheless. ''The stem of each is in a little tube that holds enough water to keep the flowers alive. If they're cut at the right time, lilies last a while.''

''Those are lilies?''

''Uh-huh. Stargazers. I use them a lot in silk arrangements for front foyers or buffets or dining room tables. They're elegant.''

He eyed her guardedly. ''You do silk arrangements?''

''No. Someone does them for me. She's the artist, but whenever I see an arrangement of fresh-cuts that I like, I make a note and tell her about it later.''

''I hate silk arrangements. They look fake.''

''Then you've never seen good ones. Good silks are hard to tell from the real thing.''

''I can tell. I can always tell.''

''You've seen that many?''

''Enough to know that it's a matter of moisture.'' His gaze fell to her mouth. ''I don't care how good the silk is, it doesn't breathe the way a real flower does. It doesn't shine or sweat. A real flower is like human skin that way.'' He brushed her cheek with the pad of his thumb, feeling the smoothness, the warmth, the dewiness that her run down the mall had brought. He also felt his own body responding almost instantaneously, so he cleared his throat, stuck his hand back into his pocket and said, "Are you hungry?"

She nodded.

"Wanna get lunch?"

"Uh-huh." She sounded breathless still.

Gideon wasn't rushing to attribute that breathlessness to anything other than the most innocent of causes, but he hadn't missed the way her eyes had widened just a fraction when he'd touched her face or the fact that she seemed glued to the spot.

He hitched his chin toward the restaurant.

With an effort, it seemed, Chris nodded again, then looked down to make sure that she had her bundle safely tucked under her arm.

"Can I carry that for you?" he asked.

"Uh, no. It's okay."

They started off. "What did you buy, anyway? Or is it a secret, maybe something black and sexy for your mom?" He faltered, suddenly wondering whether he'd put his foot in his mouth. "Uh, she's still around, isn't she?"

Chris smiled. The affection she so clearly felt for her mother brought added warmth to her eyes. "Quite. She's an energetic fifty-five. But she'd be embarrassed out of her mind to get something black and sexy. She doesn't define herself that way. No, this is for another relative. Something totally different. As a matter of fact, I don't know *what* to get my mother."

"What does she do?" Gideon asked, hoping to get hints about Chris through this mother she cared for.

"She reads, but books are so impersonal."

"What else does she do?"

"Needlepoint, but she's already in the middle of three projects and doesn't need a fourth."

"What else?"

"She cleans and cooks—" this was offered facetiously "—but I don't think she'd appreciate either a bottle of window cleaner or a tin of garlic salt."

Gideon was picturing a delightful homebody, someone he'd feel comfortable with in a minute. "How about a clay pot?"

Chris drew in her chin. "Clay pot?"

He'd seen them advertised on the back of one of the dozens of unsolicited catalogues that came in the mail every week. Rolled tight, those catalogues were kindling for his fire. Once in a while, something registered while he was doing the rolling. "You know, the kind you cook a whole meal in, kind of like a Crockpot, but clay." They'd reached the restaurant. He held the door for her to go through first.

"How do you know about clay pots?" she asked, shooting him a curious glance as she passed.

He shrugged. With a light hand on her waist, he guided her toward the hostess, who promptly led them to the quietest table in the house. Unfortunately, that wasn't saying a whole lot. The restaurant was filled, even at two, with a cross of business types from nearby office buildings and shoppers with kids. The business types were no problem, but the kids and their mothers were loud. Noting that the table the hostess had given them—a table for four, at that—was set slightly apart from the others, Gideon felt his money had been well spent. Every little bit of privacy helped when a man was pursuing his cause.

"Would you like me to hang up your coat?" he asked just before Chris slid into her seat.

She glanced at the nearby hooks. "Uh, okay." Depositing her bag and purse on one of the free chairs, she started to slip the coat off. Gideon took it from her shoulders and hung it up, then put his own jacket beside it. When he returned to the table, she was already seated. He took the chair to the right of hers, which was where the hostess had set the second menu, but no sooner had he settled in than he wondered if he'd made a mistake. Chris was sitting back in the pine captain's chair with her hands folded in her lap, looking awkward.

"Is this where I'm supposed to sit for a business lunch?" he asked, making light of it. "Or should I be sitting across from you?"

"I think," she said, glancing out at the crowd, "that if you sit across from me, I won't be able to hear a word you say. I thought most of the kids would be gone by now, but I guess at Christmastime anything goes."

"I take it you've been here before."

"Uh-huh. My family comes a lot."

"Family," he prodded nonchalantly, "as in mother and father?"

"And the rest. I'm the oldest. The youngest is just fifteen. It's harder now than it used to be, but we still try to do things together whenever we can." She opened her menu, but rather than looking at it, she took a drink of water. "The club sandwiches are good here. So are the ribs. I usually go for one of the salads. There's a great Cobb salad, and a spinach one."

"I hate spinach."

The blunt statement brought her eyes finally to his. "Like you hate silk flowers?"

"Pretty much." He paused, held her gaze, watched her cheeks turn a little pink and her slender fingers tuck a wisp of hair behind her ear. Unable to help himself, he said, "I like your outfit. You look nice in navy." He paused again. "Or aren't I supposed to say that at a business lunch?"

She looked at him for another minute, then seemed to relax. "Technically, it is a sexist thing to say."

"It's a compliment."

"Would you give a compliment like that to one of your men?"

"Like that? Of course not. He'd think I was coming on to him."

She arched an eloquent brow.

"I'm not coming on to you," Gideon told her, and in one sense it was true. He'd complimented her because he really *did* like the way she looked, and he was used to saying what he thought. "I'm just telling you you look pretty. It's a fact. Besides, I do give my men compliments. Just not like that."

"Like what, then?"

"Like . . . hey, man, that's a wild shirt . . . or . . . cool hat, bucko."

"Ah," she said gravely. "Man talk." She lowered her eyes to his shirt, then his sweater, and the corner of her mouth twitched. "I'll bet they had choice words to say about what you're wearing now."

Feeling a stab of disappointment, he looked down at himself. "What's wrong with what I'm wearing?"

"Nothing. It's a gorgeous outfit. But it's way different from what I've seen you wearing at the Rise."

It's a gorgeous outfit. Did that ever make him feel good! "Thanks, but I wasn't working in this." He snickered. "You're right. The guys would have kidded me off the lot. No, I went home to change."

She was silent, almost deliberative, for a minute before asking, "Where's home?"

"Worcester."

Her eyes went wide. "Worcester? That's halfway across the state. You're not actually commuting from there to Crosslyn Rise every day, are you?"

He nodded. "I can do it in an hour and a quarter."

"Speeding."

He shrugged.

"And you drove all that way this morning, then drove home, then drove all the way back to meet me?"

"I couldn't very well meet you in my work clothes. You wouldn't have wanted to sit across from me, much less next to me. Besides, I didn't have to drive *all* the way back. Crosslyn Rise is still farther on up."

"But I would have picked some place even closer, if I'd known." Her voice grew softer. "I'm sorry."

"Hey," he said with a puzzled smile, "it's no big thing. I asked you to name the place, and you named it." He looked around. "This is a nice place."

"Hello," the waitress said, materializing between them as though on cue. "My name is Melissa, and I'll be serving you today. May I get you something from the bar?"

Gideon raised his brows toward Chris.

She shook her head. "Tea for me, please."

"And you, sir?"

He wanted a beer, but that wasn't part of the image. Then again, he couldn't see himself ordering wine. So he settled for a Coke. "And maybe something to munch on," he said, waving his fingers a little. "What do you have?"

Chris spoke before Melissa could. "We'll have an order of skins, please. Loaded."

The minute Melissa left, he asked, "How do you know I like skins?"

"Do you?"

"Sure."

"Loaded?"

"Sure."

There was satisfaction in her smile. "So do my father and brothers, and they're all big and physical like you."

Gideon was thinking that being like her father and brothers was a good thing, since she clearly liked them, when he had a different thought. "What about your boyfriend? Does he like them?"

"My boyfriend? Oh, you mean Anthony. Uh, actually, he doesn't."

"So what does he eat when he comes here?"

"He doesn't."

"Doesn't eat?"

"Doesn't come here. He lives in Boston. And he's really not my boyfriend. Just a friend. I don't have time for a boyfriend. I told you that. I'm not interested."

"A girlfriend then?" he asked before he could think to hold his tongue.

She scowled at him. "Why *are* you so offensive." It wasn't a question.

He held up a hand and said softly, "Hey, I'm sorry. It's just that I like to know what's going on. I mean, why is a woman as beautiful and talented as you are still single?"

She threw the ball right back at him. "You're still single. What's *your* excuse?"

"I told you. I blew marriage once."

"A long time ago, you said. But you haven't tried again."

"But I date. I date a whole lot. There's just no one I like well enough to want to wake up to in the morning." He let the suggestiveness of that sink in, along with all the sexy images it brought. He could picture Chris in his bed, could picture it easily, and wondered if she could picture it, too.

She didn't look to be panting. Nor did she speak right away. Finally, slowly she said, "Then you live alone?"

He fancied he detected interest and grabbed onto the thought. "That's right."

"In an apartment?"

"A house. That I built."

A small smile touched the edge of her mouth. "Mmm. I should have guessed." She paused, seemed deliberative again. He guessed that she wasn't sure how personal to get.

"Go on," he coaxed gently. "Ask. I'll answer."

Given permission, she didn't waste any time. "You live all alone in a big house?"

"It's not big. But it's nice. And it's all I need."

"And you take care of yourself—cook, clean, do laundry?"

"I cook. I have someone come in to do the rest." He didn't see anything wrong with that. She couldn't expect that he'd do everything for himself when he had important work to do every day.

"You really do cook?"

"Enough to stay alive." He wondered what she was getting at. "Why?"

"Because you know about clay pots," she mused, and seemed suddenly, seriously pleased. "That's not a bad idea. My mother doesn't have anything like it. It's really a *good* idea. Thank you."

Gideon grinned. "Glad to be of help." Then his eyes widened at the sight of the skins that suddenly appeared on the table. They looked incredible and he was famished.

"Are you ready to order the rest?" Melissa asked.

Chris looked inquiringly at Gideon, but he hadn't even opened his menu. "Some kind of sandwich," he said softly. "You choose. You know what's good."

She ordered a triple-decker turkey club for him and a Cobb salad for herself. Then she hesitated, seeming unsure for a minute.

"Sounds great," he assured her, and winked at Melissa, who blushed and left. When he looked back at Chris, she was reaching into her purse and pulling out a notebook. Tugging a pen from its spiral binding, she opened to a page marked by a clip.

"What are you doing?" Gideon asked. He was being the gentleman, waiting for her to help herself to a potato skin before he dug in.

"I have questions for you. I want to make notes."

"About me?"

"About Crosslyn Rise."

"Oh." He looked longingly at the skins. Taking the two large spoons resting beside them, he transferred one to Chris's plate.

She protested instantly. "Uh-uh. Those are for you."

"I can't eat them all."

"Then you'll have to take them home for supper. All I want is a salad."

"Aha," he breathed, "you're one of those women who's always on a diet." He shot a quick look at her hips. "I don't see any fat."

"It's there."

"Where?"

"There." She sat back in her chair and stared at him.

Fantasize all he might, but that stare told him she wasn't saying a word about her thighs or her bottom or her waist or her breasts, if those were the spots where she imagined there was fat. So he helped himself to a skin and said, "Okay, what are your questions?" He figured that while he was eating, they could take care of business, so that by the time he was done they could move on to more interesting topics.

He had to hand it to her. She was prepared. She knew exactly what she wanted to ask and went right to it. "Will you consider putting wood shingles on the roof?"

"No." He said. "Next question." He forked half a skin into his mouth.

"Why not?"

"Mmm. These are great."

"Why not wood shingles?" she repeated patiently.

"Because they're expensive and impractical."

"But they look so nice."

"Brick does, too, but it's expensive as hell."

She held his gaze without so much as a blink. "That was my next question. Couldn't we use brick in a few select areas?"

"That's not part of Carter's concept. He wants clapboard."

"What do you think?"

"I think you should talk with Carter."

"What do *you* think?"

"I think we can do very well without that expense, too. Next question." He took another skin, cut it in two, downed the half.

"Windows. What about some half-rounds?"

"What about them?"

"They'd look spectacular over the French doors in the back."

Gideon had to agree with her there, but he was a realist. "It's still a matter of cost," he said when he'd finished what was in his mouth. "I based my bid on the plans Carter gave me. Half-rounds are expensive. If I go over budget, it's money out of my pocket any way you see it."

"Maybe you won't have to go over budget," she said hopefully, "not if you get a good deal from a supplier."

"You know a supplier who'll give us that kind of deal?"

Her hope seemed to fade. "I thought you might."

He looked down at his plate as he cut another skin, arching little more than a brow in her direction. "You're the one with connections in the business. Me, I'm on my own." He popped the skin into his mouth.

"You don't have any relatives in construction?"

After a minute of chewing, he said, "None living. My dad was a housepainter. But he's been gone for ten years now."

She sobered. "Ten years. He must have been very young."

"Not so young overall, but too young to die. There was an accident on the job. He never recovered." Gideon sent her a pointed look. "That's one of the reasons I go berserk when I see carelessness at my sites."

After a minute's quiet, she said, "I can understand that." She'd put down the notebook, had her elbows on the arms of the chair and was making no attempt to look anywhere but at him. "Were you working with him at the time?"

"No. I worked with him when I was a kid, but I was already into construction when the accident happened. He did a lot of work for me in those last years, but when he fell, it was on another job. The scaffolding collapsed."

"I'm sorry," she said, and sounded it. "Were you two close?"

"Growing up, he was all I had."

"Your mother?"

"Left when I was three."

"Just left?" Chris asked, looking appalled.

"She met someone else, someone with more promise. So she divorced my dad, married the other guy and moved to California." He put down his fork. "She did well. I have to give her that. She's become a very nice society lady—with silk arrangements all over her house.''

"Ah, but not *good* silks, if you thought they looked fake.'' She smiled for a second, then sobered again. "Do you see her often?''

"Once, maybe twice a year. She keeps in touch. She even wanted me to come live with her at one point, but I wasn't about to betray my dad that way. Then, after he died, I wasn't about to move. My roots are here. My business is here.'' He smirked. "She isn't wild about what I do. Thinks it's a little pedestrian. But that's okay. California doesn't tempt me, anyway. I'm not the beach boy type.''

Chris mirrored his smirk. "Not into surfing?''

"Not quite. Softball and basketball. That's it.''

"That's enough,'' she said with feeling.

"Your father and brothers, too?'' he guessed.

"Brothers,'' she answered. "They're basketball fanatics.''

"How about you? Are you into exercise?''

"Uh-huh. I do ballet.''

Ballet. He might have known. He had about as much appreciation for ballet as he did for Godiva chocolates. He was a Hershey man all the way. "Do you dance in shows?''

"Oh, no. Even if I were good enough, which I'm not, and even if I were young enough, which I'm not, I wouldn't have the time. I go to class twice a week, for the fun and the exercise of it. In a slow and controlled kind of way, it's a rigorous workout.'' She took a fast breath. "So why did you move from painting to construction?"

He wanted to know more about her, but she kept turning the questions back at him, which bothered him, on the one hand, because he wasn't used to talking about himself so much, at least not on really personal matters. For instance, he didn't usually tell people about his mother. Then again, Chris seemed genuinely interested, which made it easy to talk. She wasn't critical. Just curious. As though he were a puzzle she wanted to figure out.

So he'd be her puzzle. Maybe she'd be as intrigued with him as he was with her.

"Painting to construction?" He thought back to the time he'd made the switch, which had been hard, given his father's preference. "Money was part of it. The construction business was booming, while painting just went along on the same even keel. I also had a thing for independence. I didn't want to be just my dad's son. But I guess most of it had to do with challenge." He narrowed an eye. "Ever spend day after day after day painting a house? When I first started, I thought it was great. I could stand up there on a ladder, goin' back and forth with a brush, listening to my music from morning to night. Then the monotony set in. I used to feel like I was dryin' up inside. I mean, I didn't have to *think*."

"You certainly have to do that now."

"Thank you."

"I mean it."

"I know. Believe me, I *know* how much I have to think every day. There are times when it's a major pain in the butt, but I wouldn't trade what I do for any other job."

Chris looked puzzled at that. "But you've invested in Crosslyn Rise. You're a member of the consortium. Isn't that like stepping over the line?"

"I'm kind of straddling it right now."

"Then it's not a permanent move into development?"

Gideon thought about it for a minute. A month before, he'd have had a ready answer, but he didn't have one now. "I invested in the Rise because I've never invested in a project before. It was a step up the ladder, something I wanted to try, something I *had* to try." He frowned down at his plate, nudging it back and forth by tiny degrees. "So I'm trying it, and I'm finding that I really want it to work, I mean, *really* want it to work, and there's pressure that goes with that." His eyes sought hers. "Do you know what I mean?"

She nodded, but he wasn't done. "The pressure isn't all fun. And then there's the thing about working in an office, versus working at a site. I like the meetings at the bank. I like being involved at that level. But when the meetings adjourn and we all shake hands, there isn't the feeling of accomplishment that I get at the end of a day when I stand back and see the progress that's been made on a house. Or the feeling," he said, coming alive just at the thought, "of standing back and seeing the finished product, seeing people move in, seeing them live in a place I've built and loving it. I could never give up building. I could never give up that kind of satisfaction.''

He said back quietly in his chair, thinking about what he'd said, feeling sheepish. "Funny, I hadn't quite put all those thoughts into words before. You're a positive influence.''

"No,'' she said softly. "You'd have said those things, or recognized that you felt them, sooner or later. I just happened to ask the question that triggered it, that's all.''

"I'll bet you do that a lot for people. It takes a good listener to ask a good question. You're a good listener.''

She shrugged, then looked quickly up and removed a hand from the table when Melissa delivered their lunches. When they were alone again, she said, "Listening is important in my line of work. If I don't hear what a client is saying, I can't deliver." She dunked her tea bag into the minicarafe of hot water. "Speaking of which, I have more questions about Crosslyn Rise.''

"If they involve spending money—''

"Of course they involve spending money,'' she teased, her blue eyes simultaneously dead serious and mischievous.

"Then you might as well save your breath,'' he warned, but gently. "We're locked into our budget, says Ben Heavey. He's one of the men you met at the bank that night, and a tightwad? He gives new meaning to the word."

"But what if I can save money here—" she held out her right hand, then her left "—and use it there?"

He pointed his fork at her plate. "Eat your salad."

"Take the flooring. Carter's blueprints call for oak flooring throughout the place, but the fact is that in practically every home I've decorated, the people want carpeting in the bedrooms. If we were to do that, substituting underlayment for oak in the bedrooms, even just the upstairs bedrooms, with the money we'd save, we could pickle the oak downstairs. *That* would look *spectacular*."

"Pickled oak is a bitch to keep clean."

"Only if you have little kids—"

"*I'd* have trouble with it—"

"Or big kids who don't know how to wipe their feet, but how many of those will we attract at Crosslyn Rise? Think about it, Gideon. Or ask Nina Stone. She'll be the first one to tell you that we're aiming at a mature buyer. Not a retiree, exactly, but certainly not a young couple with a whole gang of kids."

"How many kids did you say were in your family?"

"I didn't. But there are six."

"Six kids." He grinned. "That's fun. From what to fifteen?"

She saw through the ruse at once and told him so with a look. "Thirty-three. I'm thirty-three. Is that supposed to have something to do with Crosslyn Rise?''

"Would you move there?"

"If I wanted to live on the North Shore, which I don't, because my business is in Belmont."

"Where do you live now?" Of the information he wanted, that was one vital piece.

She hesitated for just a minute before saying, "Belmont."

"To be near your family?"

She nodded slowly. "You could say that."

"Because you're all so close," he said quickly, so that she wouldn't think he was interested, *personally* interested, in where she lived. "Do you know how lucky you are about that? I've never had any brothers or sisters. Thanksgiving was my dad and me. Christmas was my dad and me. Fourth of July was my dad and me."

"Didn't you have any friends?"

"Sure, lots of them, and we were invited places and *went* places all the time. But that's different from being home for the holidays." He grew still, picked up his sandwich and took a bite.

Chris speared a piece of lettuce. For a minute she seemed lost in her thoughts. Then, quietly she said, "My family means the world to me. I don't know what I'd do without them."

"Is that why you haven't married?"

She raised her head. "I told you why. Marriage just isn't high on my list of priorities."

"Because you're too busy. But you made time to have lunch with me."

"This is business."

"It's also fun. At least, I think so. It's the most fun I've had at lunch in a while." It was true, he realized. He'd had more bawdy lunches, certainly wilder ones, but never one that excited him more. Even aside from the sexual attraction, he liked Chris. She was intelligent. Interesting.

Concentrating on her salad, she began to eat, first a piece of lettuce, then a slice of olive, then some chicken and a crumble of blue cheese. Gideon, too, ate in silence, but he was watching her all the while.

"Well?" he said when he couldn't stand it any longer.

She looked up. "Well what?"

"Are you enjoying yourself?"

"Right now, no. I'm feeling very awkward."

"Because I'm watching you eat?"

"Because you're waiting for me to say something that I don't want to say." With care, she set down her fork. "Gideon, I'm not looking for a relationship. I thought I made that clear."

"Well, you said it, but do I have to take it for gospel?"

"Yes."

"Come on, Chris. I like you."

"I'm glad. That'll make it easier for us to work together."

"What about after work? Can I see you?"

"No. I told you. I don't have the time or desire for something like that."

Sitting back in his chair, he gave her a long, hard look. "I think you're bluffing," he said, and to some extent he was himself. He wasn't a psychologist. He wasn't into analyzing people's motives. But he was trying to understand Chris, to understand why she wouldn't date him, when he had a gut feeling they'd be good together. "I think you're protecting yourself, because maybe, just maybe you're afraid of involvement. You've got your family, and that's great, and I imagine it's time-consuming to give a big family a hunk of yourself. But I think that if the right thing came along, you'd have all the time in the world for it—" he leaned close enough to breathe in the gentle floral scent that clung to her skin "—and more desire than a man could begin to hope for." He stayed close for a minute, because he just couldn't leave her so soon. Unable to resist, he planted a soft kiss on her cheek. Then he straightened and sat back.

"I'm not giving up, Chris." His voice was thick, vibrating in response to all he felt inside. "I'll wait as long as it takes. I've got all the time in the world, too—and more desire than you could ever want."

5

Chris never knew how she made it through the rest of lunch. She felt warm all over, her insides were humming, and even after Gideon took pity on her and changed the subject, she was shockingly aware of him—shockingly, because the things she kept noticing she hadn't noticed in any man, *any* man since she'd been eighteen years old, and even then, it was different.

Brant had been eighteen, too. He'd been big and brawny, a football player, far from the best on the team but good enough to earn a college scholarship. She remembered the nights they'd spent before graduation, parked in the shadowy grove behind the reservoir in his secondhand Chevy. She'd worshiped him then, had thought him the most beautiful creature on earth. With his sable hair and eyes, his strong neck and shoulders, and hands that knew just what to do with her breasts, he excited her beyond belief. Wanting only to please him, she let him open her blouse and bra to touch her naked flesh, and when that wasn't enough, she let him slip a hand inside her jeans, and when even that wasn't enough, she wore a skirt, so that all he had to do was take off her panties, unzip his pants and push inside her. It had hurt the first time, and she bled, but after that it was better, then better still.

Looking back, trying to remember how she could have been so taken in, she wondered if she wasn't half-turned-on by the illicitness of what they were doing. She hadn't ever been a rebel, but she was a senior in high school and feeling very grown-up in a houseful of far younger siblings. And then, yes, there was Brant. Looking back, she saw that he was a shallow cad, but at the time he was every cheerleader's dream with his thick hair, his flexing muscles, his tiny backside and his large, strong thighs.

Gideon Lowe put her memory of Brant Conway to shame. Gideon was mature, richly so, a freewheeling individual with a wealth of character, all of which was reflected in his physicality. The things she noticed about him—that stuck in her mind long after she left Joe's Grille—were the dark shadow of a mustache over his clean-shaven upper lip, the neat, narrow lobe of his ear and the way his hair swept vibrantly behind it, the length of his fingers and their strength, their newly scrubbed look, the scar on the smallest of them. She noticed the tan—albeit fading with the season—on his neck and his face, the crinkles radiating outward from the corners of his eyes, the small indentation on his cheek that should have been a dimple but wasn't. She remembered his size—not only his largeness, but the way he leaned close, making her feel enveloped and protected. And his scent, she remembered that with every breath she took. It was clean, very male and very enticing.

The problem, of course, was resisting the enticement, which she was determined to do above all else. She meant what she told him. She didn't have time for a serious man in her life. Her career was moving, and when she wasn't working, her time was happily filled with family. Thanksgiving had been larger—now that Jason was married, Evan engaged, and Mark and Steven bringing friends home from college—and more fun than ever. Christmas promised to be the same. She wanted to enjoy the holiday bustle. And then, there was work, which felt the Christmas crunch, too. Clients wanted everything delivered and looking great for the holidays. That meant extra phone calls on Chris's part, extra appointments, extra deliveries, extra installations. She *really* didn't have time for Gideon Lowe.

Of course, trying to explain that to Gideon was like beating her head against a brick wall. He called an hour after she returned to the office, on the day they met for lunch, to make sure she'd gotten back safely. He called two days later to say that, though he couldn't promise anything, he was getting estimates on half-round windows. He called three days after that to ask her to dinner.

Just hearing his voice sparked the heat in her veins. She couldn't possibly go to dinner with him. Couldn't *possibly*. "I'm sorry, Gideon, but I can't."

"Can't, or won't?"

"Can't. I have other plans." Fortunately, she did.

"Break them."

"I can't do that." The Christmas concert was being held at the high school that night. She wouldn't miss it for the world.

"Then tomorrow night. We could take in a movie or something."

She squeezed her eyes shut and said more softly, "No. I'm sorry."

He was silent for a minute. "You won't see me at all?"

"I don't think it would be a good idea. We work together. Let's leave it at that."

"But I'm lonely."

She cast a helpless glance at the ceiling. When he was blunt that way, there was something so endearing about the man that she wanted to strangle him. He was making things hard for her. "I thought you said you date. In fact, you said you date *a whole lot*." She remembered that quite clearly.

"I did, and I do, but those women are just friends. They're fine for fast fun, but they don't do anything for loneliness. They don't fill my senses the way you do."

"For *God's* sake, Gideon," she breathed. He was being corny as hell, but she liked it. It wasn't fair.

"Say you'll see me this weekend. Sometime. Anytime."

"I have a better idea," she said, trying to regain control of herself and the situation. "I'll talk with you on the phone again next week. There are questions that I didn't get around to asking you when we had lunch—'' questions that she hadn't had the presence of mind to ask after he'd leaned close and kissed her ''—and I've had other thoughts on the Rise since then. What do you say we talk a week from today?''

''A week!''

''This is an awful season for me. I'm up to my ears in promises and commitments. A week from today? Please?''

Mercifully her plea got through to him, because he did agree to call her the following Thursday. She was therefore unprepared when, on that Tuesday, between calls to a furniture factory in North Carolina, a ceramic tile importer in Delaware and an independent carpenter in Bangor, Maine, she heard an unmistakably familiar male voice coming from the outer office.

After listening to it for a minute, she knew just what was happening. She had told Margie that she needed an uninterrupted hour to make all her calls. So Margie was giving Gideon a hard time. But Gideon wasn't giving up.

Leaving her chair, Chris opened the office door, crossed her arms over her breasts and leaned against the jamb. ''What are you doing here, Gideon?'' she asked in as stern a voice as she could produce, given the way her heart was thudding at first sound, then sight of him. He was wearing jeans, a sweater and a hip-length parka. His hair was combed, but he hadn't shaved, which suggested that he'd come straight from work, with the benefit of only cursory repairs in the truck. The image of that unsettled her even more. But the worst was the way his eyes lit up when she appeared.

"Hey, Chris," he said, as though finding her here were a total surprise, "what's up?"

"What are you doing here?" she repeated, but she was having trouble keeping a straight face. For a big, burly, bullheaded guy, he looked adorably innocent.

Sticking his hands into the pockets of his jeans— knowingly or unknowingly pushing his parka in the process to reveal the faithful gloving of his lower limbs—he shrugged and said, "I was in the neighborhood and thought I'd drop in. How've you been?"

She steeled herself against his charm. "Just fine since we talked last week."

"Have a good weekend?"

"Uh-huh. And you?"

"Lonely. Very lonely. But I told you it would be." The look in his eye told her that if she didn't invite him into her office, he'd elaborate on that in front of Margie.

Chris didn't want even the slightest elaboration. She didn't trust where he'd stop, and it wasn't only Margie who'd hear, but Andrea, who was with a client in the second office and would no doubt be out before long. Then there would be comments and questions and suggestions the minute he left, and she couldn't bear that. No, the less attention drawn to Gideon, the better.

Dropping her arms, she nodded him into her office. The minute he was inside with the door closed, she sent him a baleful stare. "I told you I couldn't see you, and I mean it, Gideon. I have work to do. I'm *swamped*." She shook a hand at her desk. "See that mess? That's what the Christmas rush is about. I don't have time to play." Her eyes widened. "What are you doing?"

"Taking off my jacket. It's warm in here."

Didn't she know it. Something about the two of them closed in the same room sent the temperature soaring. She felt the rise vividly, and it didn't help that he looked to be bare under his sweater, which fell over his pectorals with taunting grace.

"Put that jacket back on," she ordered, and would have helped him with it if she dared touch him, which she didn't. "You're not staying."

"I thought we could talk about the Rise."

"Baloney. You're not here about the Rise, and you know it," she scolded, but she seemed to have lost his attention. He was looking around her office, taking in the apricot, pale gray and chrome decor.

"Not bad," he decided. Crossing to the upholstered sofa, he pushed at one of the cushions with a testing hand, then turned and lowered his long frame onto the piece. He stretched out his arms, one across the back of the sofa, the other along its arm, and looked as though he'd be pleased to stay there a week.

Chris had her share of male clients, many of whom had been in her office, but none had ever looked as comfortable on that sofa as Gideon did. He was that kind of man, comfortable and unpretentious—neither of which helped her peace of mind any more than his sweater did, or his jeans. "I have to work, Gideon," she pleaded softly.

He gestured toward the desk. "Be my guest. I won't say a word."

"I can't work with you here."

"Why not?"

"You'll distract me."

"You don't have to look at me."

"I'll see you anyway."

"Ahh." He sighed. "A confession at last."

She blushed, then scowled in an attempt to hide it. "Gideon. Please."

Coming forward, he put his elbows on his spread thighs and linked his hands loosely between his knees. His voice went lower, his eyes more soulful. "It's been just over a week since I've seen you, but it feels like a month. You look so pretty."

Chris was wearing a burgundy jumper that she'd pulled from the closet, and a simple cream-colored blouse with a large pin at the throat. It was one of her oldest outfits. She didn't think she looked pretty at all and was embarrassed that he should say it. "Please, Gideon."

But he wasn't taking back the words. "I think about you a lot. I think about what you're doing and who you're with. I think about—wonder about—whether you're thinking of me."

She shut her eyes tight against the lure of his voice. "I told you. Things have been wild."

"But when you're home alone at night, do you think about me then?"

She pressed two fingers to her lips, where, just the night before, she'd dreamed he'd kissed her. From behind the fingers, she breathed a soft, "This isn't what I want."

"It's not what I want, either, but it's happening, and I can't ignore it. I feel an attraction to you the likes of which I haven't felt in years. I've tried to hold back, Chris. I tried not to come today because I know how you feel. But I'm not real good at waiting around. Call it impatient or domineering or macho, but I'm used to taking the lead. I want to see you again."

Anthony Haskell waited around, Chris realized. Anthony waited around all the time for her to beckon him on, but when she did, there was never any heat. There was heat now, with Gideon. She felt it running from her head to her toes, stalling and pooling at strategic spots in between.

Needing a buffer, she took refuge in the large chair behind the desk. "I thought we agreed to talk on Thursday," she said a little shakily.

"We did. And we can. But you're right. I didn't come to talk about the Rise. And I don't really want to talk about it on Thursday. There's nothing pressing there, certainly nothing that can't wait until the beginning of January, especially if you're as busy now as you say."

"I *am* busy."

"I believe you," he said genially. "But you have to take a break sometime. Why can't you take one with me?"

"I don't *want* to."

"Why not?"

She could think of dozens of answers, none of which she was ready to share.

Gideon didn't have that problem. "Don't you like me?"

She scowled. "Of course, I like you. If I didn't, I'd have already called the police to kick you out. You're interfering with my business."

"Do I still make you nervous?"

"Not nervous. Exasperated. Gideon," she begged, "I have to work."

"Do I excite you?"

"Yeah, to thoughts of mayhem." She glowered at him. "This isn't the time or place for a discussion like this."

"You're right. Let me take you to dinner tonight."

She shook her head.

"Tomorrow night, then. Come on, Chris, you have to eat."

"I do eat. With my family."

"Can't they spare you for one night?"

She shook her head.

"Then let me come eat with you." He seemed to warm to the idea once it was out. "I'd like that. I mean, I'd really like it. Big family dinners are something I always wanted but never had. I'll bring flowers for your mom. I'll bring cigars for your dad—"

"He doesn't smoke."

"Then beer."

"He doesn't drink."

"Then cashew nuts."

She shook her head. "Sorry. Doctor's orders."

Gideon looked appalled. "The poor guy. What does he *do* for the little joys in life?"

"He sneaks out to the kitchen when he thinks none of us is looking and steals kisses from my mom while she does the dishes."

That shut Gideon up. For a minute he just stared at her as though he couldn't grasp the image. Then his expression slid from soft to longing. "That's nice," he finally said, his voice a little thick. "I'm envious of you all."

Chris was beginning to feel like the worst kind of heel. If she was to believe Gideon's act, he was all alone in the world. But he dated, he dated *a lot*. And he had a mother in California. Maybe even a stepfamily. No doubt there would be numerous brightly wrapped gifts under his Christmas tree. So why did he look as though spending a little time with her family might be the best gift of all?

"Look," she said with a helpless sigh, "my parents have a Christmas open house every year." It would be packed. She could do her good deed, ease her conscience and be protected by sheer numbers. "It's this Sunday. If you want, you could come."

He brightened. "I'll come. Tell me where and when."

Taking a business card—deliberately, as a reminder of the nature of their relationship—she printed the address on the back. "It runs from three to seven, with the best of the food hitting the table at six."

"What should I wear?" he asked as he rose from the sofa to take the card.

"Something casual. Like what you wore to lunch last week."

He looked at the card, then stretched a little to slide it into the front pocket of his jeans. Chris was barely recovering from the way that stretch had lengthened his body when he turned, grabbed his coat and threw it on. For a split second his sweater rose high enough to uncover a sliver of skin just above his jeans. In the middle of that sliver, directly above the snap, was a belly button surrounded by whorls of dark hair.

She felt as though she'd been hit by a truck.

Oblivious to her turmoil, Gideon made for the door. Once there, he turned and gave her an ear-to-ear grin. "You've made my day. Made my *week*. Thanks, Chris. I'll see you Sunday." With a wink, he was gone.

Five days was far too soon to see him again, Chris decided on Sunday morning as she pulled on a sweatshirt and sweatpants and went to help her mother prepare for the party. He was still too fresh in her mind—or rather, the effect he had on her was too fresh. Every time she thought of him, her palms itched. Itched to touch. Itched to touch hair-spattered male flesh. And every time she thought of doing it, she burned.

She didn't know what was wrong with her. For fifteen years, she hadn't felt the least attraction to a man, and it hadn't been deliberate. She was with men when she worked. Her dad had men over. So did her brothers. But none had ever turned her on, it was as simple, as blunt as that.

What she felt for Gideon Lowe made up for all those chaste years, so much so that she was frightened. She sensed she'd need far more than crowds to lessen the impact he had on her. She only prayed he'd arrive late to coincide with the food. The less time he stayed, the better.

Gideon would have arrived at three on the nose if it hadn't been for his truck, which coughed and choked and balked at having to go out in the cold. He called it every name in the book as he worked under its hood, finally even threatened to trade it in for a sports car. That must have hit home, because the next time he tried it, the engine turned smoothly over and hummed nicely along while he went back into the house to scrub his hands clean.

It was three-thirty when he pulled into the closest spot he could find to the address Chris had written down. The street was pretty and tree lined, though the trees were bare, in a neighborhood that was old and well loved. Wood-frame houses stood, one after another, on scant quarter-acre lots. Their closeness gave a cozy feeling that was reinforced by wreaths decorating each and every door and Christmas lights shining from nearly every window. None of the houses was large, including Chris's parents', but that added to the coziness.

From the looks of things, the party was in full swing. The front door was open, there were people preceding him up the walk, and the side stoop was occupied by a group of college-age kids who seemed oblivious to the cold.

Leaving his truck, he followed the walk to the door, dodging two young girls who darted out of the house to join their friends. Once on the threshold, he felt a little unsure for the first time since he'd bulldozed the invitation from Chris. He'd gone to parties at the homes of people far more wealthy and influential, but none mattered more to him than this one.

He assumed that he was looking a little lost, because he barely had time to take more than two steps into the house when he was greeted by a tall gray-haired man. "Welcome," the man said in a voice loud enough to be heard above the din. "Come on in."

Gideon extended his hand. "Mr. Gillette?"

"That I am," the man said, giving him a hearty shake, "but probably not the one you want. I'm Peter. If you're looking for my brother Frank, he's mix-

ing the eggnog, which is real serious business, so I'd
advise you to leave him be. If he messes up, we all lose
out, if you get my drift.''

''Actually,'' Gideon said, searching for a blond
head among those crowded into the living room, ''I'm
looking for Christine. I'm a friend of hers, Gideon
Lowe.''

''Even better,'' Peter said with a broad grin. ''Tell
you what. Why don't you hang your coat up in the
closet while I go find her.''

Gideon was already working his way out of the
leather jacket. ''That's okay. I'll go.'' Spotting a hook
at the end of the closet, he freed himself of the jacket.
''Which direction?''

Peter looked first toward the dining room on the
left, then the living room on the right, then back toward the dining room. ''The kitchen, I guess. If she's
not helping Frank, she'll be helping Mellie.'' He
pointed through the dining room. ''That way.''

With a nod, Gideon started off. The dining room
was filled with people helping themselves to drinks and
the small holiday cookies and cakes that covered plate
after plate on the table. At one end was a huge punch
bowl, into which a man Gideon assumed to be Frank
was alternately pouring eggnog and brandy. He was a
good-looking man, Gideon thought, tall and stocky,
with salt-and-pepper hair and a ruddy complexion.
Despite the good-natured coaxing and wheedling of
several onlookers, he was concentrating solely on his
work.

Gideon inched between two people here, three others there, until he'd made his way to the far end of the dining room and slipped through the door into a small pantry that led to the kitchen. There he saw Chris. She was standing at the counter by the sink with her back to him. Beside her was the woman who had to be her mother, if the similarity of height, build and coloring were any indication. They were slicing hot kielbasa, putting toothpicks in each slice, arranging the slices on a platter.

Coming up close behind Chris, he bent and put a gentle kiss beneath her ear.

She cried out and jumped a mile, then whirled on him in a fury. "Gideon! Don't *ever* do that again! My God—" she pressed her hand to her heart "—you've aged me fifteen years."

He gestured toward her mother, who was eyeing him curiously. "If this lovely lady is any indication of what you'll look like fifteen years from now, you've got it made." He extended his hand toward Mellie. "Mrs. Gillette?" There was no mistaking it. The eyes were the same, the hair, the mouth. Chris was slimmer and, wearing loose pants with a tunic top, more stylishly dressed, but they were very definitely mother and daughter.

"Gideon . . . ?"

"Gideon Lowe, Mom. He's the builder for Crosslyn Rise and may well be the death of me before I even get to the project." She scolded him with her eyes, then her voice. "I thought you were coming later."

"You suggested six if I was starved. I figured I'd give myself a while to build up to that." He shook Mellie's hand warmly.

"It's nice to meet you, Mr. Lowe."

"Gideon. Nice to meet you, too, ma'am." He let her take her hand back and return to her work. "This is quite some party." He looked down at the platter. "Can I help?"

"No," both women said at the same time.

Chris elaborated. "Men don't cook in my mother's kitchen. My father does the eggnog, but not in here. Men are good for cleaning up. That's all."

"And a few other things," Mellie added softly, almost under her breath. Then she looked straight at Gideon and spoke up, "But I don't want you in here. You're a guest. Christine, leave these now. I'll finish up. Take Gideon out and introduce him around."

Gideon thought Chris was going to argue, but even he could see that Mellie wasn't taking no for an answer. So she washed and dried her hands, then led him through another door into a hallway that led back to the front. This hallway, too, was crammed with people, giving Gideon ample excuse to stay close to Chris.

"You look fantastic," he murmured into her ear as they inched their way along.

"Thanks," she murmured back.

"You taste even better."

"Oh, please," she whispered, but before he had a chance to come back with anything wickedly witty, she half turned, took his elbow and drew him alongside her. "Gideon, this is my brother Steven. He's a junior at U. of Mass. Steven, meet Gideon Lowe, a builder I work with."

Gideon shook hands with a blond-haired young man who also had the family features. "You must be one of the basketball fanatics," he said, noting that Steven stood nearly as tall as he did.

Steven grinned. "You got it. You, too?"

"You bet. If not for this gorgeous sister of yours, I'd be at the game right now." Leaning close, he asked out of the corner of his mouth, "Any fix on the score?"

In every bit as low a tone, Steven answered, "Last time I checked, the Celts were up by eight. Game's on upstairs, if you want."

Gideon slapped his shoulder and straightened. "Thanks for the word. Maybe later."

"Don't you dare go up and watch that game," Chris warned, leading him on by the hand. "That would be very rude."

"Keep holding my hand," he whispered, "and I'll stay right by your side." He raised his voice. "Ah, here comes another brother."

Chris shot him an amused grin. "This is Jason. He works with Dad. His wife's over there—" She stood on tiptoe, looking around, "Jase, where's Cheryl?"

Jason shook hands with Gideon. "Upstairs nursing the baby."

"Gideon Lowe," Gideon said. "What baby?"

"A little boy," Chris explained. "He's their first."

"Hey, congratulations."

"Thanks," Jason said, but he had something else on his mind. "Chrissie, you seen Mark? He parked that rattletrap of his in the driveway in back of the Davissons and they have to leave."

"Try the front steps. Last I knew he was holding court out there." Jason promptly made for the door, but before Chris and Gideon could make any progress, a loud cheer came from the dining room. Seconds later, a grinning Frank Gillette emerged through a gauntlet of backslapping friends. When he caught sight of Chris, his eyes lit up even more.

"Go on in and try it, honey. They say it's better than ever."

"I will," Chris said. Her hand tightened on Gideon's. "Dad, I'd like you to meet Gideon Lowe. He and I work together."

"Nice to meet you," Frank said, "and glad you could come."

"It's kind of you all to welcome me."

"Any friend of Chrissie's, as they say. Hey, Evan," he called, "get over here." Seconds later, he was joined by another fair-haired son. "Evan, say hello to Gideon Lowe. Gideon, this is my second oldest son, and his fiancée, Tina."

Gideon smiled and nodded to them. Waving, they continued on into the living room. Gideon was beginning to wonder how Chris kept her brothers apart when yet another stole by. This one was younger and faster. He would have made it out the front door if Frank hadn't reached out and grabbed his arm. "Where you off to so fast?"

"I want to see Mark's friends. Steve says there're a couple'a cool girls out there."

Chris grinned up at Gideon. "That's Alex, the baby."

Alex looked instantly grieved. "Come on, Chris. That's not fair. I'm fifteen. Besides, I'm not the baby. Jill is."

"Jill?" Gideon asked. Chris had said there were six kids in the family. He was sure he'd already met ten. "There's another one?"

"Yeah," Alex said, "and there she is." He pointed to the girl coming down the stairs. While everyone looked that way, he escaped out the door.

"Come over here, girl," Frank said, but it was to Chris's side that the girl came.

Accordingly Chris was the one to make the introduction. "Say hi to Gideon," she told Jill. "He's the builder for Crosslyn Rise, but be careful what you say. He's also on the consortium."

Jill grinned. "Ah, he's the one?"

"He's the one."

Gideon couldn't take his eyes off Jill. With her long brown hair and her large brown eyes, she was different from every other Gillette he'd met. A beauty, she looked to be at least seventeen, yet Alex had called her the baby, and he was fifteen. Gideon wondered if they were twins, with Jill the younger of the two by mere minutes. She couldn't possibly be *fourteen*.

He stuck out his free hand. "Hi, Jill."

For a split second she seemed a little shy, and in that second he almost imagined she could be younger. Then she composed herself and gave him her hand, along with Chris's smile. "Nice to meet you."

"The pleasure's mine. It's not often that I get to hang around with *two* gorgeous women."

Chris arched a brow at Jill. "Didn't I tell you?"

Grinning back, Jill nodded.

"What?" Gideon asked.

"You know how to throw it around," Jill said.

Gideon looked at Frank. "Was that bull? Are these two women gorgeous, or are they gorgeous?"

"They're gorgeous," Frank confirmed, "but who'm I to judge. I got a vested interest in them."

Gideon considered that interest as he looked from Chris's face to Jill's and back. "All those blondes and one brunette," he said to no one in particular. To Jill he said, "How old are you?"

"Fifteen."

To Chris, he said, "I thought Alex was fifteen."

"He is."

"Then they're twins?"

"Not exactly."

"Irish twins?"

Chris slid an amused glance at Jill before saying, "No. Jill is five months younger."

"Five months?" He frowned. "No, that can't be—" He stopped when Chris and Jill burst out laughing, then looked questioningly at Frank, who was scowling at Chris.

"That's not real nice, Chris. I told you not to do it. It isn't fair to put people on the spot like that."

"Thank you," Gideon told him, and directed his gaze at Chris. It was Jill, though, who offered the explanation he sought.

"I'm not his," she said, tossing her dark head toward Frank. "I'm *hers*." Her head bobbed toward Chris.

Hers? For a long minute, Gideon didn't make the connection. When he did, he ruled it out as quickly as it had come.

Chris squeezed his hand, which she hadn't let go of once. She was looking up at him, her eyes surprisingly serious. "Say something."

Gideon said the first thing that came to mind. "You're too young, and she's too old."

"I was eighteen when she was born."

"You look like sisters."

"If she were my sister, she'd be blond."

"But she has the Gillette smile."

"That's my smile. She's my daughter."

Daughter. Somehow, the word did it—that, and the fact that with two witnesses, one of whom had originally made the claim and the other of whom wasn't opening his mouth to rebut it, Gideon figured it had to be true. "Wow," he breathed. "A daughter."

"Does that shock you?"

"Yeah," he said, then felt it worth repeating. "Yeah."

"Kind of throws things into a new light?" Chris asked, but before he could answer, she released his hand, said a soft, "Excuse me, I want to check on Mom," and escaped into the crowd.

"Chris—"

Frank put a tempering hand on his arm. "Let her go. She'll be back."

But Gideon's eyes continued to follow her blond head as it moved farther away. "She'll misinterpret what I just said. I know she will. She'll think I don't want any part of her because she has a child, but that's not what I'm feeling at all. I'm feeling that, my God, she's done this wonderful thing in life, and I haven't ever done anything that even comes *close* in importance to it."

"This is getting heavy," Jill drawled.

Gideon's eyes flew to hers. He'd forgotten she was there, and was appalled. "Hey, I'm sorry. I didn't mean to offend you, too. I really like...your mom. If you're her daughter, I like you, too. Hell, I like the whole damned family. I don't have *any* family."

Jill's eyes widened. "None?"

But before he could answer, there was an uproar at the door. Frank turned around, then, wearing a broad grin, turned back and leaned close to Gideon. "See that bald-headed son of a bitch who just walked in? I haven't seen him in twenty years.'' To Jill, he said, ''Take Gideon around, honey. If you run out of things to say, point him toward the game. He's a fan.''

''Chris said I couldn't,'' Gideon told him.

Frank made a face. ''Mellie says I can't, but do I listen?'' Slapping his shoulder, he went off to greet his friend.

''You don't have *any* family?'' Jill repeated, picking up right where she'd left off.

He shook his head. His hand felt empty without Chris's, so he slipped it into his pocket.

''No family.''

''That's awful. Do you live all alone?''

''All alone.''

''Wow, I don't think I could do that. I'd miss having people around and things happening.''

Gideon was trying to think back to what Chris had said about herself. There wasn't a whole lot. She had evaded some questions and turned others right back to him. He didn't think she had ever lied to him, per se, but she'd obviously chosen every word with care.

When it came to where she lived, he had the distinct impression that she had her own place close to her family's. He suddenly wondered whether, there too, she'd stretched the words. ''You don't live *here*, do you?''

''Oh, no. We're next-door. But we're here all the time.''

"Next-door?" He was trying to remember what that house had looked like. "To the right or the left?"

"Behind. We're in the garage."

"The *garage*."

She nodded. "Uh-huh."

"You're stuck in the *garage*?"

She shot him a mischievous grin. "Want to see?"

"Yeah, I want to see." It occurred to him that Chris's daughter was a treasure trove of information on Chris, and that he wasn't adverse to getting what he could.

Jill led him around the crowd at the door, out and across the frozen lawn to the driveway. "My friends love my place," she said when he'd come up alongside her. "They keep bugging their parents to do something like it for them."

From what Gideon could see, the garage was like any other. Detached from the house, it was set far back at the end of a long driveway, with a single large door that would raise and lower to allow two cars inside. His builder's mind went to work imagining all the possibilities, but when Jill opened a side door and beckoned him inside, he wasn't prepared for what he found.

The garage had been elongated at the rear and converted into a small house, with an open living-room-kitchen-dining area, then a balcony above, off which two doors led, he assumed, to bedrooms. To compensate for a dearth of windows, there were indirect lights aplenty, as befitted the home of the daughter and granddaughter of an electrician. But what impressed Gideon even more than that was the decor. Nearly everything was white, and what wasn't white was a soft shade of blue. There was a light, bright, clean feel to the place. He couldn't believe he was in a garage.

"This is fantastic," he said.

Jill beamed. "Mom designed it, and Gramp's friends did it. I was just a baby and Mom was still in school, so it meant she could leave me with Gramma and Alex during the day, then have me to herself here at night."

Gideon was still looking around, taking in the small, sweet touches—like pictures of Jill at every imaginable age, in frames that were unique, one from the other—but he heard what she said. "So you grew up right alongside Alex?"

"Uh-huh. He's not bad for an uncle."

Gideon looked at her to find a very dry, very mature grin on her face. Narrowing an eye, he said, "You get a kick out of that, don't you?"

"Kinda." She dropped onto the arm of a nearby sofa with her legs planted straight to the floor. "People don't know what to think when they meet Alex and me. I mean, we're in the same grade and we have the same last name but we look so different. They don't believe it when we tell them the truth. They get the funniest looks on their faces—like you did before."

He wondered what explanation she gave for where her own father was. He wanted to ask about that himself, but figured it was something better asked of Chris. "Do you mind your mom working?"

Jill shrugged. "She has to earn a living."

"But you must miss her."

"Yes and no. I have Gramma. She's always around. And I have a house full of uncles. And then Mom comes home at night and tells me about everything she did at work that day."

"Everything?"

Jill nodded. "We're very close."

He had the odd feeling that it was a warning. Cautiously he asked, "What did she say about me?"

Without any hesitancy—as though she'd been wanting the question and he'd done nothing more than follow her lead—she said, "That you were a builder, that you were on the committee that interviewed her, and that you were a real jerk." When Gideon's face fell, she burst out laughing. "Just kidding. She didn't say that. She did say that you were very good-looking and very confident and that she wasn't sure how easy it'd be working with you." Jill paused, then added, "She likes you, I think."

"I know she likes me—"

"I mean, *likes* you."

Gideon studied her hesitantly. "Think so?" When she nodded, he said, "How do you know?"

"The way she ran off after we told you about me. She was nervous about what you'd think. She wouldn't have been if she didn't care. And then there was the thing with the hands."

"What thing?"

"She was holding yours. Or letting you hold hers. She doesn't usually do that with men. She's very prim."

"But you noticed the hands."

"I sure did."

Gideon ran a finger inside the collar of his shirt. "How old did you say you were?"

"It was only hands," she said in a long-suffering way. "And I *ought* to notice things like that. She's my mother. I care about what she does with her life."

He could see that she did, and had the oddest sense of talking with Chris's parent rather than her child. "Would it bother you if I dated her?"

"No. She ought to have more fun. She works too hard."

"What about Anthony?"

"Anthony is a total dweeb."

"Oh." That about said it. "Okay. Then he isn't competition?"

"Are you kidding?" she said with a look of such absurdity on her face that he would have laughed if they'd been talking about anything else. But his future with Chris was no laughing matter.

"So we rule out Anthony. Are there any others I should know about?"

"Did she say there were?"

"No."

Jill tipped her head. "There's your answer."

"And you wouldn't mind it if I took her out sometimes?"

The head straightened and there was a return hint of absurdity in her expression. "Why would I mind?"

"If I took her out, it would be taking her away from time spent with you."

Jill didn't have to consider that for long. "There are times when I want to do things with friends, but I feel so guilty going out and leaving Mom alone here. She can go over to the house and be with everyone there, but it's not the same. I mean, I love her and all, but my friends go shopping or to the movies on the weekends, and it's fun to do that. And then there's college. I want to go away. I've never *been* away. But how can I do that if it means leaving her alone?"

Gideon scratched his head. "Y'know, if I didn't know better, I'd wonder whether you're trying to marry her off."

"I'm not," Jill protested, and came off the sofa. "I wouldn't be saying this to just anyone, but you like her, and she likes you, and what I'm saying is that you can't use me as an excuse for not taking her out. I'm a good kid. I don't drink or do drugs or smoke. I'll be gone in three years. I won't be in the way."

Gideon hadn't had much experience with fifteen-year-old girls, but he knew without doubt that this one had a soft and sensitive side. She might be totally adjusted to the fact of her parentage; she might be far more mature than her years. But only in some respects. In others, she was still a girl wanting to please the adults in her life.

The fact that she considered him one of those adults touched him to the core. Crossing to where she stood, he tipped her chin up and said, "You could never be in the way, Jill. I don't know what'll happen between your mother and me. Our relationship has barely gotten off the ground. But believe me when I say that your existence is a plus. A big, big plus. I've been alone most of my life. I *like* the idea of being with someone who has family."

"Family can get in the way sometimes."

"You wouldn't say that if you've been without the way I have."

"Are you gonna tell Mom that?"

"As soon as I can get her alone long enough to talk."

"What's going on here?" Chris asked from the door.

Jill slipped away from his hand. "Whoops. Looks like you'll have that chance sooner'n you thought." She grinned. "Hi, Mom. I think I'll go back to the house and get something to drink. I'm parched." She was halfway past Chris when she said, "Invite him for Christmas dinner. He's nice." Before Chris could begin to scold, she was gone.

6

"Whose idea was it to come back here?" Chris asked. She wasn't quite angry, wasn't quite pleased. In fact, she wasn't quite sure *what* she was feeling, and hadn't been since she'd shocked Gideon with the fact of Jill.

"Uh, I'm not sure. I think it was kind of mutual."

"Uh-huh." Chris understood. "It was Jill's idea. You're protecting her."

Gideon held up a cautioning hand. "Look, she may have suggested it, but only after I started pestering her about where you two lived." Dropping the hand to his pocket, he looked around. "It's a super place, Chris. I like it a lot."

"So do I, but it's only a place. Jill's a person. She means more to me than anything else on earth. I don't want her hurt."

Gideon straightened. "You think I could *hurt* her?"

That was exactly what Chris thought. "You could get real close, then lose interest. When I said that she throws a new light on things, I meant it."

"Hold on a minute. I'm not romancing Jill. It's you—"

"But she's part of the package," Chris interrupted, feeling the urgency of the message. "That's what I'm trying to tell you. You say you want to date me. You hoodwinked me into inviting you here today. Well, okay, you're here, and I'll date you, but you have to know where my priorities lie. I'm not like some women who flit around wherever the mood takes them. I'm not an independent agent. I'm not a free spirit."

"I never thought you were," Gideon said soberly. "From the start, you've been serious and down-to-earth. You made it clear how much your family means to you."

"Jill is more than family. She's someone I created—"

"Not alone."

"Someone I *chose* to bring into this world. I have a responsibility to her."

"And you think you're unique?" Gideon challenged impulsively. "Doesn't every mother feel that responsibility? Doesn't every single mother feel it even more strongly, just like you do? For God's sake, Chris, I'm not trying to come between you and your daughter. Maybe I'm trying to add something to both of your lives. Ever thought of it that way? I sure as hell know I'm trying to add something to mine." He swore again, this time under his breath. "*Trying* is the operative word here. You get so goddamned prickly that I'm not making a helluva lot of headway." He stopped, then started right back up in the next breath.

"And as far as Jill's existence throwing a new light on things, let me tell you that I find the fact that you have a daughter to be incredibly wonderful—which you would have known sooner if you hadn't run off so fast. You do that a lot, Chris. It's a bad habit. You run off before things can be settled."

"There's nothing to be settled here," Chris informed him, staunchly sticking to her guns, "since nothing's open for discussion. Jill is my daughter. For the past fifteen years, she's been the first thought on my mind when I wake up in the morning and the last thought before I fall asleep at night."

"Is that healthy?" Gideon asked innocently, but the words set her off.

"Healthy or not, that's the way it is," she snapped. "A woman with a child isn't the same as one without. You ought to think really hard about that before you do any more sweet-talking around here." She turned and made for the door, but Gideon was across the floor with lightning speed, catching her arm, drawing her back into the living room and shoving the door shut.

"Not so fast. Not this time. This time we talk."

"I can't talk now," she cried. "I have a house full of Christmas guests to entertain."

But Gideon was shaking his head. "Those guests entertain themselves, and besides, there are a dozen other hosts in that house." His voice softened, as did his hand on her arm, though he didn't release her.

"Just for a minute, Chris. I won't keep you long, but I want to make something very clear."

She glanced up at him, and her heart lurched. The look in his eyes was gentle, almost exquisitely so.

"I like you," he said. "God only knows why, because you give me a hard time, but I like you a lot. You could've had *five* kids, with half of them in diapers, and I wouldn't care. Knowing about Jill now, I respect you even more for what you've done with your business, and you've obviously done something right with her, or she wouldn't be as nice a kid as she seems to be." He paused. "When I said I was shocked back there, it was because you never let on—I didn't expect it. You just didn't strike me as the type to—"

"Get knocked up?"

"Have a baby so young. Okay, yeah, maybe be with a guy so young." A tiny crease appeared between his brows. Quietly he asked, "Who was he?"

"It doesn't matter," Chris said, and tried to turn back toward the door only to have Gideon lock a grip on her other arm, too.

"Did you love him?" he asked, still quietly, even unsurely.

Chris had been prepared for criticism, which was what she'd gotten most often when she'd first become pregnant. *Didn't you know what you were doing? Didn't you use anything? Didn't you stop to consider the consequences?* Rarely had she been asked what Gideon just asked her. Looking up into his deep charcoal eyes, she almost imagined he was worried.

"I thought I did," she told him in a voice as quiet as his. "We were both seniors. He was handsome and popular, full of charm and fun. I was totally snowed. We didn't have anywhere to go, so we used to park up behind the reservoir. That's where Jill was conceived."

She thought Gideon started to wince, but he caught himself. "What happened after?"

"He didn't want me or the baby," she said bluntly. She'd long since passed the time when she blamed herself for that. She might have loved Brant at the time, or thought she did, but the only person Brant had loved was himself. "He denied it was his."

This time Gideon's wince was for real. "What kind of selfish bastard was he?"

Chris shrugged. "He was going to college on a scholarship and didn't want anyone or anything to slow him down."

"So he left you in the lurch. You must have been furious."

"Furious, hurt, frightened."

"I'd be angry still."

"Why? I got the better part of the deal. I got Jill."

Gideon seemed momentarily stunned, as though that idea had never occurred to him. Finally, in a hoarse whisper, he said, "That's what I think I like about you so much. You feel things. You love."

Chris too was stunned, nearly as much by his whispered awe as by the reverence in his eyes. Then she didn't have time to think of either, because he lowered his head to kiss her. At least, that was what she thought he was going to do. She felt the approach of his mouth, the warmth of his breath—then he pulled back and looked at her again, and in the look, something gave inside her.

"Do it," she whispered, suddenly wanting his kiss more than anything else.

His lips were smooth and firm. They touched hers lightly, rubbed them open in a back and forth caress, then, just as his hands left her arms and framed her face, came in more surely.

Chris was overwhelmed by the warmth of the kiss, its wetness, and by Gideon's fresh male scent that seemed to fill her and overflow. Needs that had lain dormant for better than fifteen years suddenly came to life, touching off an explosion of awareness inside her. Her limbs tingled, her heart pounded, her blood rushed hot through her veins. Feeling dizzy and hungry at the same time, she clasped fistfuls of sweater at his waist, gave a tiny moan and opened her mouth to his silent demand.

The demand went on and on, sometimes pressing, sometimes hovering, sometimes sucking so strongly that she was sure she'd never emerge whole again. When, with several last, lingering touches, the kiss ended, she felt bereft.

It was a minute before she realized exactly what had happened, and by that time, Gideon had his mouth pressed to her temple and his arms wrapped tightly around her. With her slow return to reality came the awareness of a fine tremor snaking through his large frame.

"Gideon?" she whispered, shaky herself.

"Shh," he whispered back. "Give me a minute."

She knew all too well why he needed the time. She could feel the reason pressing insistently against her thigh, and while the strength of it shocked her, it also excited her beyond belief. She wanted another kiss. She wanted some touching. She wanted something even harder, something to relieve the deep ache she was feeling.

"I knew it'd be like that," he whispered again.

"I didn't know it *could* be."

He made a low, longing sound and crushed her even closer.

"That's not helping," she whispered, but neither was breathing against his neck the way she was doing. His skin was firm and hot and smelled wonderfully of man.

"I know, but I need it. I can't let you go just yet."

"You'll have to soon. Someone's apt to come looking."

Raising his head, he caught her eyes. His voice remained little more than a ragged train of breath. "Know what I'd do if I had my way?" When she shook her head, he said, "I'd back you right up to that door and make love to you here and now."

She felt a searing heat deep in her belly and had to swallow before she could get a word out. "You can't."

"Yes, I can. I'm hard. Can't you feel?" Slipping his hands to her bottom, he manipulated her hips against his. His arousal was electrifying.

She had to close her eyes against its force. "Don't, Gideon," she cried, her breath coming in shallow gusts. She lowered her forehead to his throat.

His mouth touched her ear. "Right against that door. Then, after that, on your bed. You've never done it on a bed, have you?"

"No." She tugged at his sweater, which she was still clutching for dear life. "Don't talk."

"Why not?"

"Because you're making things harder."

"I'll say," he muttered with the nudge of his hips.

Moaning against the fire that small movement sparked, she slipped her arms around his neck, drawing herself up on tiptoe, and hung on tight. Her body felt foreign but wonderful. It knew what it wanted. Her mind wasn't so sure. "I have to get back to the house."

"You don't want to."

"I have to." But she moved against him, needing the friction to ease the knot between her legs.

"You want to stay here and make love with me."

"Oh, Gideon!" she cried.

"You do. I'd make it so good, baby, so good. I wouldn't rush you, wouldn't hurt you, and it'd be so incredibly good." He slipped a hand from her bottom to her thigh, then moved upward and inward.

"Don't," she begged, but the plea was empty. Between his words and his closeness, she was floating, then soaring, burning up from the inside out. When he touched her where she was most sensitive, she cried out, and when he began to caress her, she held on tighter to his neck.

"You're so hot here," he whispered.

"Gideon," she moaned. "Oh, no." She was arching into his hand, coming apart with no way to stop it.

His stroking grew bolder. "That's it, baby. That's it. Feel it. Let it come."

She was lost. In a moment of blinding bliss, she convulsed into an orgasm that left her gasping for air. She couldn't speak, could only make small, throaty sounds. Gradually they eased. The next sound she made was a humiliated sob. Twisting away from Gideon with such suddenness that he was taken off guard, she stumbled around the sofa and collapsed into its corner, pressing her knees together and huddling low over them.

"It's okay, sweetheart," Gideon said, reaching out to stroke her hair.

She felt his hand and would have pulled away if there was anywhere to pull to. "That shouldn't have happened," she cried. "I'm so embarrassed."

Barely removing his hand, Gideon came around the end of the sofa and squatted close before her. "Don't be," he said. "I'm not. I feel so *good*."

"You can't feel good. You didn't . . . get anything."

"Wrong. Way wrong. I got a whole lot." His strong hands were framing her neck, and his voice, though hoarse, was astonishingly tender. He leaned forward so that his breath brushed her cheek. "Was that the first time since—"

She gave a sharp, quick nod against her knees.

"The first time since Jill's father?"

She repeated the same sharp nod.

"You've never done it yourself?"

She kicked his leg.

"Chris?" When she didn't answer, he said again, "Chris?"

Her voice was small. "What?"

"I think I'm falling in love with you."

"Don't *say* that."

"But it's true."

She pressed her hands to her ears and shook her head.

Forcibly removing her hands, he raised her head until she was sitting up, looking at him. "I won't say it again, if it makes you uncomfortable. It shakes me a little, too. We don't know each other much, do we?"

Unable to take her eyes from his, she gave a feeble shake of her head.

"But there's a remedy for that," he went on. "You can stop cooking up cockamamy excuses for why you can't see me."

Chris pulled back as much as his hands would allow. "They're not cockamamy excuses. This is the busiest time of the year for me. Between work and all the things I want to do with Jill—"

"Invite me along. We don't have to be alone all the time."

She made a disbelieving face. "What kind of man wants to put up with that?"

His voice went low and husky again. "The kind of man who knows his woman is made of fire. As long as I know it's coming, I can wait."

Chris felt her cheeks go red. "I won't ever live that down, will I?"

"Not if I can help it. It was the most beautiful, most sensual, most natural and spontaneous response I've ever experienced with a woman."

She had to look away. His eyes were too intense. Very softly she said, "You've been with lots of women, haven't you?"

"Over the years? Enough." He paused. "But if it's the health thing that's got you worried, don't be. I've always used a rubber. Always. For birth control, as much as anything. I'm clean, Chris."

Focusing on a cable twist in his sweater, she murmured. "I wasn't worried about that." She was actually worried about the issue of experience, because, other than with Brant, she was very much without.

"I don't want to use anything with you."

Her eyes shot to his. "You have to. I don't have— I'm not taking—"

His mouth cut off the words, kissing her gently, then less gently, before he regained control and drew up his head. "If you got pregnant by me, I wouldn't run away. I'd want you and the baby and Jill and your family. I'd marry you in a minute."

Chris was having trouble breathing again. "This conversation is very premature."

"Just so you know how I feel."

"How can you feel that way so soon?"

"Beats me, but I do."

"I think you're getting carried away on some kind of fantasy."

"No fantasy. Just you."

How was she supposed to answer *that*? She swallowed. "I have to get back to the house."

Gideon sat on his heels. "I'm staying till the party's over. Can we talk more then?"

"Maybe we shouldn't. Maybe we should let things cool off a little."

"It won't help. The fire's there, whether we're together or not. It's there even when I sleep. I had a wet dream last night—"

"Gideon, for goodness' sakes!"

"I did."

"But don't *tell* me."

"Why not?" he asked reasonably. "I know damned well you're going to think back on what happened here and be embarrassed, and I just want you to know that you're not the only one who loses control sometimes. You had far more reason to than I did, what with the way I was touching you—"

She pressed a hand to his mouth. "Please," she begged in a whisper, "don't say another word." She waited. He was silent. She moved her fingers very lightly over his lips. "I'm going to get up now and go back to the house. If you'd like, you can come, too. You can talk with people—Jessica and Carter may be here by now—or even watch the game if it isn't over."

"The Lakers come on next," he murmured against her fingers.

"Okay. The Lakers. My brothers will be watching. You can get something to eat and stay as long as you want, but I can't go out with you afterward. I want to help my mother clean up. Then I want to spend some time with Jill. Then I want to go to bed. Tomorrow's as busy as Mondays get." Her hand slid from his mouth to the shirt collar that rose above the crew neck of his sweater.

"What's on for tomorrow night?"

"I have deliveries to supervise until eight."

"So Jill will be here with your folks?"

"She has Driver Ed on Monday nights. I'll pick her up on my way home."

"What about supper?"

"I'll grab something when I get home."

"Why don't I pick up Chinese and stop by your office?"

"Because I won't be at my office."

"So I'll go where you are."

"You can't. Not with food. My clients would die."

"Okay. What about Tuesday night? No, forget Tuesday night. I have a game." His eyes lit up. "Come see me play."

For an instant, he was so eager that she actually wished she could. But the logistics wouldn't work. "In Worcester?"

"Too far, hmm?"

"And I have ballet."

"Okay. What's on for Wednesday night?"

"Jill's piano recital."

"I'll come."

"You will not. She's nervous enough at recitals without having to worry about her mother's new boyfriend showing up."

Gideon grinned. "New boyfriend. I like that. It's better than the builder." His grin vanished. "But I won't make her nervous. She likes me."

"She likes you here, now, today. That's because you're one of lots of people coming to party. She's apt to be threatened when she realizes something's going on between us."

"She already does. And she won't be threatened. She *likes* me. Besides, she wants you to date. She told me so."

"She told you?"

"Yes."

Chris felt just the slightest bit betrayed. "What else did she tell you?"

"Not much. You came along before she had a chance. But, damn it, Chris, we haven't settled anything here. When can I see you again? We're up to Thursday."

"Thursday's no good. I have ballet again, and then we're going shopping."

"I'll go with you."

But she shook her head. Last-minute Christmas shopping was something that had become almost traditional with Jill and her. Chris wasn't ready to let someone else intrude.

"Okay," Gideon said, "that brings us to the weekend, and to Christmas Eve. So are you inviting me over, or what?"

Chris didn't know what to do. Christmas Eve, then Christmas Day were every bit as personal and special and traditional for the whole family as last-minute shopping was for Jill and her alone.

"Jill said you should," he reminded her.

"Jill was out of line."

"What are all your plans?"

"Dinner, caroling, then Midnight Mass on Christmas Eve, and a huge meal on Christmas Day."

"Is it all just family?"

"No," Chris answered truthfully. "Friends come, too." She sighed and sent him a beseeching look. "But this is happening too fast, Gideon. Can't we slow it down?"

"Some things won't be slowed down—like what happened a little while ago."

She squeezed her eyes shut.

"What are you afraid of, Chris? What's holding you back?"

She had asked herself the same question more than once in recent weeks. Slowly she opened her eyes and met his. "Being hurt. I'm afraid of that. Jill may be the highlight of my life, but what Brant did hurt. I got over it. I came back and built a life, and I think I've been a great mother. Things are going smoothly. I don't want that to change."

"Not even for the better?"

"I don't *need* things to be better."

The look on Gideon's face contradicted her even before he spoke. "I think you do. There's a closeness only a man can give that I think you crave. It's like the way you held my hand back at the house, and the way you came apart before, even the way you're touching me right now."

"I'm not—"

"You are. Look at your hand."

Chris did. Her hand was folded over his collar, her fingers against the warm skin on the inside. Very carefully she removed them and put her hand into her lap. "I didn't know I was doing that," she said meekly.

"Like I didn't know what was happening until I woke up panting this morning. There's something to be said for the subconscious. It's more honest than we are sometimes."

He had a point, she supposed. She could deny that she wanted him, deny that she wanted any kind of relationship, but it wouldn't be the truth. Still, despite his arguments, she meant what she'd said about slowing things down.

"New Year's Eve," she said, focusing on her lap. "You probably already have plans—"

"I don't, and I accept. What would you like to do? We can work around Jill's plans or your family's plans. Just tell me. I'm open."

Hesitantly she raised her eyes. "Jill is going to a party at a friend's house. I have to drop her there, then pick her up. She's bringing two other friends home for a sleep-over."

"A sleep-over? Wow, that'd be fun!"

"Gideon, you're not invited to the sleep-over."

"So what *do* I get?"

"Four hours, while she's at the party. We could go somewhere to eat, maybe dance. Or we could go to First Night."

"First Night is loud and cold and crowded. I vote for the other."

"We may have trouble getting reservations this late."

"I don't want reservations. I want to eat here."

She didn't know whether to laugh or cry. "I didn't *invite* you to eat here."

"But it makes sense, doesn't it?" he argued. "Go to a restaurant on New Year's Eve, and it's crowded and overpriced and slow. You'll be nervous about getting back in time, so you won't be able to relax. On the other hand, if we eat here, we can talk all we want.

We really need to do that, Chris, just talk. Besides, if we go somewhere fancy, I'll have to go shopping. You've already seen the sum total of my fancy wardrobe, and I hate shopping. Don't make me do it, not until after Christmas at least.''

"If you hate shopping, why did you offer to go with Jill and me?''

"Because that would be fun. It's shopping for *me* that I hate.''

She was bemused. "Why?''

"Because it's so damned hard to get things that fit. I'm broad up here, and long down there, so things have to be tailored, which means having some salesclerk feel me up.''

She sputtered out a laugh. "That's terrific.''

"No, it's sickening. Anybody feels me up, I want it to be you. So what do you say? Dinner here on New Year's Eve? Nice and quiet and relaxed? I'll bring some food if you want. Better still, give me a list and I'll pick up groceries so we can make dinner together. Now *that's* a good idea.''

Chris had to admit that it was. She wasn't a big one for public New Year's Eves and had always spent hers quietly. The idea of being with Gideon for those few hours while Jill was at her party was appealing.

"Okay,'' she said.

He broke out into a smile. Standing, he tugged her to her feet and wrapped an arm around her waist as he started for the door. "What time should I come? Four? Five?''

"Try eight-thirty." Jill's party began at eight. That would give Chris time to come home, change, get things ready.

"No way am I waiting around until eight-thirty, when everything closes at midafternoon. Five-thirty. I'll come at five-thirty. Then I can talk with Jill before she leaves."

"Jill will be totally preoccupied with her hair."

"So I'll be here to tell her how great it looks."

"Come at seven-thirty. You can go with me when I drive her to the party."

"Six. We can have appetizers early."

"Seven, and that's the earliest, the absolute earliest you can come."

"Can I bring champagne?"

"Wine. I like it better. And wear your fancy outfit. Is that the one you were wearing that day at the bank?" She wanted to see it again. Even through her nervousness his handsomeness that day had registered.

"Yeah," he protested, "but that defeats the purpose of staying in."

She shook her head and said softly, "It's New Year's Eve. If we're having a nice dinner with wine, we have to dress the part. And don't say I've already seen it, because I don't work that way. You don't have to wear something different every time you see me. I'm not that shallow."

"I didn't say you were. But it's me. My pride."

"Your pride is misplaced if you're hung up on clothes. Wear the blazer and slacks."

"The blazer and slacks?"

"Yes."

He sighed, gave her a squeeze and opened the door. "Okay. The blazer and slacks it is." He inhaled a hearty breathful of the fast-falling winter's night. "Wow, do I feel good."

Chris was surprised to realize that she did, too.

The feeling persisted. On the one hand, she could say it was the Christmas spirit. Her family always made the holiday a happy time. Deep down, though, she knew there were other reasons this year. Jill was happy. The business was going well. And Gideon had come on the scene.

He didn't let her forget that last fact. He called her every night, usually around ten, when he knew she'd be home, and though he never kept her on the phone for long—just wanted to see how her day had been or tell her something about his—the calls were sweet.

Jill was aware of them. She was the one who sat by the phone doing her homework when the ring pierced the quiet night, or talking with a friend when the call-waiting clicked. Sometimes Chris took the call in the same room, sometimes in another room. Each time, Jill acknowledged it afterward.

Not that Chris would have tried to hide anything. She knew that if she wanted Jill to be open and communicative with her, she had to be the same way right

back. Their relationship had always been honest that
way. And besides, there wasn't anything to hide. Gideon
liked her. So he was calling her.

Of course, Jill wanted to know more. "Do you like
him?" she asked, wandering down to the kitchen after
one of the calls.

In a burst of late-night energy, Chris was making
wreath cookies, which required a minimum of brain
and a modicum of brawn. She was vigorously stirring
the butter and marshmallows that she'd unceremoniously
dumped into a pot.

"He's nice," she answered. "I didn't expect him to
be after what happened at the Rise that first day."
She'd told Jill about that when it happened, albeit
more philosophically than she'd felt at the moment of
confrontation. "So I'm surprised. But I still don't
know him very well."

"It sounds like he wants to change that."

"Uh-huh." Chris felt the same shimmer of excitement
she always felt when she anticipated seeing Gideon
again.

"Why isn't he coming for Christmas?"

Chris kept stirring. "Because I didn't invite him."

"Why not?"

"Because he's too new. Christmas is for people
we're really close to. Our family is special. If you're
not one of us, you have to *earn* a place at our table."
She'd been trying for a little dry wit. It went right past
Jill.

"But he's alone. He'll be sitting there in a lonely apartment all by himself. He probably doesn't even have a tree."

Chris felt a moment's unease, wondering just how thickly Gideon had poured it on. If there was one thing she wouldn't abide, it was his using Jill to get to her. "Did he mention a lonely apartment?"

"No, but he said he had no family."

"Okay, that's true. But he doesn't live in an apartment, to begin with. He lives in a house that he built himself—"

"So he's sitting in a lonely house."

"He is not. Jill, he has lots of friends. I'm sure he's doing something with them." She hadn't asked, exactly, but she assumed that was the case. He was a really friendly guy, and he said he dated, he dated *a lot*. Chris didn't believe that he'd left all of his holiday time free.

Of course, he would have come for Christmas if she'd invited him, and he jumped at her first mention of New Year's Eve, so apparently whatever plans he had weren't etched in stone. She didn't want to think a woman was involved, didn't want to think he would break a date and disappoint someone. Better, she decided, to imagine that if he wasn't with her, he'd be with a large group of friends.

Maybe some of his workmen.

Maybe his basketball teammates.

She wondered what he wore on the court and how he looked.

"Do you think you could like him?"

Brought back from a small distance, Chris stirred the melting marshmallows with greater force. The roughness of the wooden spoon against the bottom of the pot told her that there was some sticking, apt punishment for a wandering mind. "I do like him. I told you that."

"Love him?"

Though she couldn't help but remember what Gideon had said about falling in love with her, Chris shook her head. "Too soon. Way too soon. Ask me that in another year or two."

"That's not how love happens. It happens quickly."

"Says the authority. Sweetheart, I forgot to take out the food coloring. Can you get it for me? Green?"

Jill took the small vial from the baking supply shelf and removed its lid. "How many drops?" She held it poised.

"Start with four."

Jill squeezed. Chris stirred. Gradually the thick white stuff turned a faintly minty shade.

"A little more, I think."

Jill squeezed, she stirred, but if she had hoped Jill would let the matter of love go, she was mistaken.

"You loved my father when I was conceived."

"Uh-huh." They had discussed that at length several years before, when Chris had sat down with Jill and explained what getting a period was about. Given the slightest encouragement, Jill had asked questions about making babies and making love. She knew who her father was, that he had left Massachusetts before her birth, that he was selling real estate in Arizona. At that time, she had wanted to know about Chris's relationship with him.

Chris had been forthright in telling her about feeling love and the specialness of the moment. She never wanted Jill to feel unwanted, though in essence Brant had made it clear that she was. His whole family had moved away—conveniently, a job transfer had come through for his father—and, to Chris's knowledge, none of them had been back. Outside of family, few people knew who Jill's father was.

"But you'd only been dating him for two months."

"I was young. When you're young, you're more quickly taken with things like love. Another drop, maybe?"

Jill added it, while Chris kept stirring.

"Don't you think it's more romantic when it's fast? I mean, I think what happened to you was *really* romantic. You saw each other in English, started doing homework together, fell in love and did it. Do you think he's married now?"

"Probably."

"Do you think he ever wonders about me?"

Chris sent her an affectionate smile. "He must. You're that strong a being."

"Think he ever wants to see me?"

"I think he doesn't dare." She tried to keep it light. "Seeing you, he'll realize all he's missed. He'll hate himself."

Jill frowned. "But what kind of parent isn't curious about his own child?"

Chris had asked herself that question dozens of times, and in many of those times she'd thought the lowliest things about Brant. But she'd vowed many years ago not to bad-mouth him in front of Jill. "The kind who may not be able to forgive himself for leaving you behind. He knows you exist. I imagine—" it was a wild guess, giving Brant a big benefit of the doubt "—that knowledge has been with him a lot."

Jill thought about that, standing back while Chris dumped the premeasured cups of corn flakes into the pot with the melted marshmallows that were now a comfortable Christmas green. Finally Jill said, "Do you ever imagine that you might open the front door one day and find him there?"

"No." That was the last thing Chris wanted. She had no desire to see Brant, no desire to have Brant see Jill. Jill was *hers*. She felt vehemently about that. For Jill's sake alone, she tempered her feelings. "He's probably very involved with his own life. His family only lived here for three years. They were midwesterners to begin with. They have no ties here."

"That didn't mean he couldn't have married you if he loved you."

Chris had to work hard stirring the mess in the pot, but she appreciated the physical demand. It was a good outlet. "He had plans. He was going to college. He had a scholarship."

But Jill was insistent. "If he loved you, he could have married you."

Her petulance, far more than the words themselves, stopped Chris. Leaving the wooden spoon sticking straight up, she turned and took Jill's face in her hands. "Then I guess he didn't love me," she said softly, "at least, not as much as I thought. And in that sense, it's a good thing we didn't get married. The marriage wouldn't have been good. We'd have been unhappy together. And you would have suffered." She paused. "Do you miss having a father so much?"

"No. Not so much. You know that." They'd talked about it before. "There are times when I wonder, that's all. There are times when I think it would be nice to go places, just the three of us."

"So what would Gramma and Gramps do?" she teased. "And Alex? And the others?"

Jill thought about that for a minute, gave a small smile of concession and shrugged, at which point Chris planted a kiss in the middle of her forehead. She was about to turn back to the pot when Jill said, "I still think you should have invited Gideon for Christmas dinner."

"Uh-oh. We're on this again?"

"It was just a thought."

"Well, here's another one. I think that sticky stuff in the pot may have hardened. You gonna clean up the mess?"

In a blink, Jill was the picture of innocence. "Me? I still have homework to do." She slipped smoothly away and was up the stairs before Chris could think to scold. Not that she would have. All too soon, Jill would be slipping smoothly away to college, then beyond. Chris wasn't about to scold away their time together, not when it was so dear.

7

Come New Year's Eve, Chris wasn't thinking of spending time with Jill, but spending time without her. Christmas with the family had been wonderfully fun and absorbing—her mother had *loved* the clay pot—but in the week that followed, in all the little in-between moments when her mind might have been on something else but wasn't, Chris thought of Gideon. Each time, she felt a warm suffusion of desire.

He continued to call every night, "just to make sure you don't forget me," he teased, which was a laugh. She couldn't have forgotten him if she'd tried. He was like a string tied around her finger, a tightness around her insides, cinching deeply and pleasantly.

Had anyone read her mind during that week, she would have been mortified, so carnal were her thoughts. Rather than picturing Gideon in his blazer and slacks, she pictured him in every state of undress imaginable. It didn't help that she was haunted by glimpses of a sliver of skin, a whorl of dark hair and a belly button. When he called at night, she pictured him lying in bed wearing briefs, or nothing. She pictured his body, pictured the dark hair that would mat it, clustering more thickly at some places than others. She pictured him coming to her on New Year's Eve, unbuttoning his shirt, removing it, opening his pants, removing them, baring himself to her, a man at the height of his virility and proud of it.

At times, she wondered if there was something wrong with her, if she was so sex starved that anyone would do. But the courier, who stopped by the office several times that week and was very attractive, didn't turn her on. Nor did her hairdresser, who was surprisingly straight. Nor did Anthony Haskell, who called several times wanting to see her and whom she turned down as gently as she could.

She didn't remember ever feeling quite so alive in quite as feminine a way as she did with the approach of New Year's Eve. Like an alarm that kept going off every few minutes, the buzz of arousal in the pit of her stomach had her counting the minutes until Gideon arrived.

Seven, she had told him. Fortunately, she was ready early, because when the bell rang at six-forty-five, she had no doubt who it was. Pulling the door open, she sent him a chiding look.

He shrugged. "I left extra time in case there was traffic, but there wasn't."

How could she get angry when the mere sight of him took her breath away? He was wearing a topcoat with the collar up against the cold, and between the lapels she caught sight of his blazer and slacks, but he looked far more handsome than he had that day at the bank.

No doubt, she decided, it had to do with the ruddy hue on his cheeks.

That hue bemused her. "You look like you've been out in the cold." But he'd been in a heated car.

"Had the windows open," he said, not taking his eyes from her. She looked bright, almost glowing, sophisticated, but young and fresh. He decided that the young part had to do with her hair. Rather than pinning it in its usual knot, she'd left it down. It was shiny and smooth, swept from a side part, its blunt-cut ends dancing on her shoulders. "It was the only way I could keep my mind on the road."

She didn't have to ask where his mind would have been otherwise. The hunger in his eyes answered that quite well. It made her glad that she'd splurged on a new dress, though the splurging hadn't been painful. Contrary to Gideon, she loved to shop. She kept herself on a budget, but she'd been due for a treat. His appreciation made the effort more than worth it.

"May I come in?" he asked.

She blushed. "Of course. I'm sorry. Here, let me take that." She reached for the grocery bag he held in one arm. They had agreed that he would bring fresh French bread and some kind of dessert, since there was a bakery not far from his house. But he held tight to the bag and, instead, handed her the two bottles of wine that he was grasping by the neck with the fingers of one hand. She peered suspiciously at the bag, which seemed filled and heavy. "What's in there?"

"I got carried away," he confessed, thinking about sweets for the sweet and other trite expressions, but loath to voice them lest she think him a jerk. Elbowing the door shut behind him, he headed for the kitchen. He set the bag on the counter, relieved her of the wine and stood it beside the bag, then gave her a slow up and down.

"You look great," he said in an understatement that he hoped his appreciative tone would correct.

Her temperature was up ten degrees, making her words breathy and warm. "Thanks. You, too." Feeling a dire urge to touch him, she laced her fingers together in the area of her lap. "Please, take your coat off." When he'd done so, she hung it in the closet, then turned to find him directly behind her.

"Where's Jill?" he whispered.

"Upstairs," she whispered back.

"Does she know I'm here?"

"She must have heard the bell."

"Do we have time for a kiss?"

"If it's a quick one."

"I don't know if I can make it quick. I've been dreaming about it for more than ten days." His whisper was growing progressively rough. He felt desperately in need. "What I had in mind was something slow and deep and wet—"

"Hey, you guys," came Jill's full voice from halfway down the stairs. She trotted down the rest, her steps muted by the carpet. "What're you whispering about?"

Chris felt she'd been caught in the act of doing something naughty. It was a minute before she could compose herself enough to realize that she hadn't— and that even if she had, she was the mother and had that right. "Gideon was saying things that *definitely* shouldn't be heard by tender ears such as yours," she drawled, and made for the kitchen. "Do me a favor, sweetie? Keep him company while I get these hors d'oeuvres?"

Gideon put his hands into the pockets of his blazer and angled them forward to hide his arousal from Jill. "Can I help?" he called after Chris. To Jill, he said, "You may think I'm one of those helpless males, but believe me, I'm not. I'm a very handy man to have around the house. I know how to crack eggs, whip cream and brew coffee."

"We could've used you around here earlier," Jill said. "Mom ruined two batches of stuffed mushrooms before she finally got one that was edible. They're supposed to be her specialty. So she thought she knew the ingredients by heart, only she blew it. That was the first time. The second time she burned the meat."

"Distracted, huh?" Gideon asked, pleased by the thought.

"You could say that." She took a step back. "How do I look?"

He checked her over. "Spectacular. Great jeans skirt. Great sweater. Great legs. Is this a boy-girl party you're going to?"

She tossed a glance at the ceiling. "Of course! I am old enough for that, y'know."

He knew all too well. Where he'd grown up, fifteen-year-old girls did far more than go to parties. Instinct told him, though, that Jill wasn't that way. Common sense told him that Chris wouldn't have stood for it. "You're gonna knock 'em dead," he told her, feeling a pride he had no right to feel. "And your hair looks great, too."

"I'm not done with my hair."

"But it looks perfect."

"It looks blah," she maintained, drawing up a thick side swath with two fingers. "I think I need a clasp or something. And some earrings. Mom—" she called, only to be interrupted when Chris approached.

"No need to yell. I'm right here." To Gideon she said apologetically, "They weren't hot enough. They'll be ready in a minute."

"I need something large and silver, Mom."

"For her hair and ears," Gideon prompted in a soft voice to Chris, who was looking a bit helplessly at Jill.

"The last time I lent you something silver," she said, thinking of a bangle bracelet that she hadn't seen in months, "I didn't get it back. You can borrow something *only* if it's returned in the morning."

"She's so fussy," Jill said to Gideon. Then she turned and went back up the stairs, leaving Gideon and Chris momentarily alone.

Gideon started whispering again. "How long do you think she'll stay up there?"

"Five seconds," Chris whispered back.

Jill yelled down, "Can I wear the enamel hair clip you bought at the Vineyard last summer?"

"I thought you wanted something silver," Chris called back.

"But the enamel one has earrings to match."

"It also," Chris murmured for Gideon's benefit, "cost an arm and a leg. She's been wanting to wear that set since I bought it. I think she's taking advantage of the company and the night."

"You can always tell her no," Gideon suggested.

Chris snorted softly, then called to Jill, "If you're very, very, *very* careful." She caught Gideon's eye. "Don't look at me that way."

"Are you always such a pushover?"

"No. But we're talking a hair clip and some earrings here. If she asked for a quart of gin, I'd say no. Same for cigarettes or dope, if I had either around the house, which I don't. The way I see it, you have to pick and chose your battles."

Gideon considered that, then nodded. "Sounds right." He shot a glance over her shoulder toward the stove. "Think your mushrooms are hot yet?"

"It's only been a minute since I last checked."

"Check again," he said, and ushered her to the farthest reaches of the kitchen. Once there, he backed her to the counter, lowered his head and captured her lips in what would have been a deep, devouring kiss had not Jill's call intruded.

"Mom?"

With a low groan, he wrenched his mouth away and stepped back.

Chris felt she was spinning around, twisting at the end of a long, spiraling line. She was hot, dizzy and frustrated. It was a minute before she could steady herself to answer. "Yes?"

"Where *is* the set?"

Chris made a small sound and closed her eyes for a minute. Then, shaking her head, she sent Gideon an apologetic look and pushed off from the counter. Jill was at the top of the stairs.

"Just tell me where it is," she called down.

But Chris didn't remember exactly where it was. "I'm coming," she said lightly. Once upstairs, it took several minutes of searching through drawers before she finally located the clip and earrings. She handed them over with a repeat of the warning, "You'll be very, very, *very* careful."

"I will. See?" She held the earrings in her hand. "They're perfect with what I'm wearing."

Chris knew that just about anything would go with a blue denim skirt. But Jill had a point. The swirls of blue-and-green enamel picked up the color of her sweater beautifully.

Rubbing her hands together, she took a deep breath. "Okay. Are you all set now? Anything else you need?"

"Nope. Thanks, Mom."

"If you're using my perfume—" which happened often "—remember, a little goes a long way. You don't want to hit the party smelling like a whorehouse."

"Okay."

"I'll be downstairs. Come on down when you're ready and have some hors d'oeuvres."

"If there are any left. Gideon looks hungry."

You should only know, Chris thought, then was grateful Jill didn't. Too soon, she'd be into serious dating. Too soon, she would know about hunger, about the urges that drove men and women together at times that weren't always the wisest. What Chris had done with Brant sixteen years before hadn't been smart at all, though she'd never had cause to regret having Jill. She meant what she'd told Gideon, that she was happy with her life.

Would she be happier with a man in the picture? She didn't know. She did know that she was drawn to Gideon in an elemental way that refused to be ignored. She was older and wiser. Still, she was drawn. Even now, returning to the kitchen to find that he'd opened the wine and was filling two glasses, she felt a flare of excitement. For a split second, she was at the end of that truncated kiss again, spinning on a spiral of desire, feeling the frustration.

"Is Jill all set?" he asked, handing her one of the glasses.

"Uh-huh."

"To us, then," he said, raising the other.

Chris touched her glass to his, then took a sip. "Mmm. This is nice." Focusing on the amber liquid, she whispered, "Sorry about before. The timing was unfortunate."

"Did I complain?" he whispered back, coming in close to her side. "It just lengthens the foreplay, that's all."

Chris felt a soft shuddering inside. "Uh, maybe we ought to sit down."

"Maybe we ought to have something to eat."

"Right." Setting her wine on the counter, she put on mitts and removed the tray of mushrooms from the oven. She arranged half of them on a dish that also held a wedge of cheese and some crackers, then put the rest back. "So they'll stay warm."

Gideon carried the dish to the low glass table in front of the living room sofa. When Chris joined him there, he popped a mushroom into his mouth. "Whoa," he drawled when it was gone, "that was worth two wasted batches."

Chris went red. "I wasn't paying attention to what I was doing."

"Like my men weren't that day at Crosslyn Rise?" he teased, because he couldn't resist, and leaned close. "Was I the cause of your distraction?"

She focused on his tie, which was silk and striped diagonally in blue, yellow and purple. "Of course not. I was thinking about work."

"I'm work, aren't I?"

"Not actively. Not yet."

"I got some half-rounds."

Her eyes flew to his, wide and pleased. "You did?"

He nodded. "Above the French doors, like you wanted. Put them in last week."

"All those phone calls, and you didn't tell me?"

"I wanted to surprise you." His gaze fell to her mouth and stuck there. "Thought if I saved it for a special time, it might win me a kiss." His voice was rough. "How about it?"

Without a moment's hesitancy, Chris reached up and put a soft kiss on his mouth. Then, because it had been so sweet and too short, she followed it with a second.

"You smell good," he whispered against her lips. "I'll bet you smell like this all over." When she caught in a small gasp, he sealed it in with the full pressure of his mouth, giving her the kind of hard, hungry kiss he craved.

Chris wanted the hardness and more. She opened to the sweep of his tongue, but he was barely done when he ended the kiss. She felt she was hanging in midair. "What's wrong?"

"Too fast," he whispered, breathing heavily. "Too hot." He shot a glance toward the stairs. "Too public." Pulling away from her, he bent over, propping his elbows on his knees. The low sounds that escaped his throat as he tried to steady his breathing told her of his discomfort.

Chris felt dismayed. In the moment when he'd kissed her, she'd forgotten that Jill was still upstairs. "I should have realized," she whispered.

"Not your fault alone. It takes two to tango."

It was a figure of speech, but she latched on to it as a diversion from desire. "Do you tango?"

"Nope. Can't dance much at all. But I make love real good."

She moaned, picturing that with far too great an ease. In desperation, she reached for the dish of mushrooms. "Here. Have another. And tell me what else is happening at the Rise."

With a slightly shaky but nonetheless deep breath, Gideon straightened. He ate another mushroom, then a third. "These are really good." He glanced back toward the kitchen. "And something else smells good." He frowned, trying to identify it.

"Rock Cornish Hens," she said. "It's the orange sauce that you smell." But she wasn't feeling at all hungry for that. "Tell me about the Rise," she repeated. She needed to think of something settling.

Gideon understood and agreed. He really hadn't intended to start things off hot and heavy. It had just happened. For both of them. But the civil thing was to talk and visit and eat first.

Casually crossing an ankle over his knee as he would have done if he'd been with the guys, he began to talk. He told Chris about the progress his crew had made, the few problems they'd run into, the solutions they'd found, that they'd moved inside. The diversion worked. When Jill joined them some fifteen minutes later, they were involved in a discussion of staircase options.

"You look great, honey," Chris told her with a smile.

"Better than great," Gideon added. "Those poor guys won't be able to keep their hands off you."

Chris shot him a dirty look. "They'd better." To Jill, she said, "One swift kick you know where."

Jill seemed embarrassed. She glanced at Gideon before sitting close to Chris and saying quietly, "My hair looks awful."

"Your hair looks great."

"I should have had it cut."

"If you had, you'd be tugging at the ends to make it longer."

"It never curls the way I want. I've been fiddling with it for an hour, and it's still twisting the wrong way."

"You're the only one who knows that. To everyone else, me included, it looks great."

"You're just saying that because you're my mother."

"I'm not your mother," Gideon said, "and I say it, too."

Jill eyed him warily. "You'd say anything to please Mom."

"No way," he argued. "If you'd been down sooner, you'd have heard me telling her that she could grovel all night if she wanted, but I was not putting in winding staircases at Crosslyn Rise.''

"This man," Chris told Jill, "is a cheapskate. There's a huge winding staircase in the mansion. It would be *perfect* to have smaller versions in the condos. Don't you think so?"

Jill crinkled her nose. "Winding staircases are good for long, sweeping dresses, but modern people don't wear them."

"That's right," Gideon chimed in. "They spend their money on skylights and Jacuzzis and Sub-Zero refrigerators instead. Face it, Chris, you're outvoted."

But Chris shook her head. "I still think they'd be great, and I'm the decorator."

"Well, I'm the builder, and I say they're too expensive. We can't fit them into the budget. That's all there is to it."

"You won't even *try*?"

"We're talking *ten grand* per staircase! I just can't do it."

Chris sensed that she could argue until she was blue in the face and she wouldn't get anywhere. She arched a brow Jill's way. "So much for trying to please me."

Jill's gaze bounced from Chris to Gideon and back. "Did I cause that fight?"

"Of course not—"

"It wasn't a fight—"

"You both look pretty ticked off—"

"I'm not ticked off—"

"I never get ticked off—"

"Maybe you shouldn't be talking work on New Year's Eve."

"I don't know—"

"Yeah, well—"

Jill looked at her watch. "Hey, can we leave now?"

"Have something to eat first," Chris told her, escaping into the role of mother with ease.

"They'll have food at the party."

"Uh-huh. Pizza, but not for a few hours, I'd wager."

"They'll have munchies," Jill argued, and rose to get her coat. "We're picking up Jenny and Laura on the way, so they can put their stuff right in the car." She grew hesitant, again looking back and forth. "Uh, whose car?"

"My Bronco," Gideon said, "if that's okay with you. And it's fine about the stuff. We'll bring it in when we get back here."

Chris hadn't known they were picking up the two other girls and sensed that it had been a last-minute deal. She wondered if it had anything to do with Gideon being there, or more specifically, with the fact that Chris was seeing him. None of Jill's friends had ever seen Chris with a man. Maybe Jill wanted her friends to know that her mother was human.

Oh, she was human, all right; human and female. Once in the truck, sitting in the front seat with Gideon, she was as keenly aware of him as she'd been back in the house. Each move he made seemed to register.

Fortunately, he kept up a steady conversation with Jill, asking about the party, who was going, who of those going she was closest to. That led into a fast discussion about school, what she was taking, what she liked best and worst. By the time they reached Jenny's house, Chris had picked up several tidbits even she hadn't known.

Jill and Jenny talked softly in back from there. They were soon joined by Laura, who directed Gideon the short distance from her house to the one where the party was being held. When they arrived, and Jenny and Laura climbed out, Jill hung back for a minute.

"So, you guys are going back home for dinner?"

"Uh-huh," Chris said.

"You're not going out to a movie or anything later?"

Chris gave her cheek a reassuring touch. "We'll be home. If there's any problem, just call and we'll be right here. Otherwise, we'll be back to pick you up at twelve-thirty." She kissed her. "Have a super time, honey."

"You, too, Mom," Jill said softly, then raised her voice. "You, too, Gideon."

"Thanks, Jill. Have fun. We'll be back."

With the slam of the door, she was gone. She glanced back once on the way to join her friends, then disappeared with them into the house.

"Was that nervousness?" Gideon asked as he shifted into gear and started off.

"I'm not sure. I think so. She's so grown-up in some ways, then in others..."

He knew just what she meant. Jill was physically mature. She was personable and poised. But the look in her eye from time to time told the truth. "She's only fifteen. That's pretty young."

"Sometimes I forget. We're such good friends."

"She's a really nice girl." He reached for Chris's hand, needing her warmth. "Even if she did interrupt what was promising to be one of the best kisses of my life."

Chris closed her fingers around his, but she didn't say a word. Left hanging, of course, was the fact that they could resume that kiss the minute they got home without worry of interruption.

"What are your parents doing tonight?" he asked a drop too casually. He was thinking of interruptions, too, but it seemed crass to let on. Hadn't he decided that they should talk and eat first?

"They're having dinner with friends. There's a local group that's been spending their New Year's Eves together for years. It used to be Mom and Dad would make a point to be home before midnight to be with us—Jill and me and anyone else who was home—but everyone's out this year."

"Except you," he said softly.

"Except me." She held more tightly to his hand. When he gave a tug, she slid closer to him.

"Are *you* nervous?" he asked. He supposed it was a form of talk, though it was getting right to the point.

She studied his face. Muted in the dark, his expression was strangely dear. "A little."

He drove quietly for a time before saying, "Does it help to know I am, too?"

"You? Buy why?"

"Because you're special. I want to make things good for you."

A light tremor shimmered through her insides. Swallowing, she said, "I think you could do that with your eyes closed."

"I don't want them closed. There's too much to see."

Like frames of a movie, the images that had haunted her flicked one after another through her mind. "Uh, Gideon?" she whispered. "I think there's something you should know."

"Don't tell me you're a virgin."

"I'm not, but—"

"You've had a baby, Chris."

"I know that," she said quickly, quietly, putting her cheek against his arm, "but the sum total of my experience with a man took place in the back seat of a '72 Chevy."

He was amused by that. "The back seat, eh?"

"It was dark. I didn't see much."

"I never did it in a car." Most everywhere else when he'd been younger, but never in a car. He'd gotten too big too fast. "What was it like?"

"That's not the point."

"But I want to know." He flattened her hand on his thigh and held it there. "Wouldn't I have to be kind of crunched up?"

"Gideon—"

"I'm too tall for a car."

She sighed. "No, you're not. You could do it. It'd just take a little ingenuity."

He began moving her hand around. "Like with positions?"

She nodded, still against his arm. She was picturing the wildest things. "You'd have to be kind of half on, half off the seat."

"I'd be on top?"

That was the only position Chris had ever known, but she'd read of others. "Or under," she murmured.

"Would we be undressed?"

"Just . . . vaguely."

"Could I touch your breasts?"

She sucked in a breath. "If you wanted to."

"Bare? Could I open your bra?"

"It might be cold."

His low voice, angled into her hair, was like liquid fire, which was precisely what was searing his gut. "I'd want to do it anyway. I want to see what you look like all over, then I'd warm you up."

She pressed her face into his arm. "Gideon—"

He slid her hand upward, urging it back and forth at the very top of his thigh. "Heating up?"

"Oh, yes."

"It doesn't take much with us."

"I know. I don't understand it. All these years, and I haven't been attracted to any other man." But she could feel the heat in him searing her palm and curling right through her. Later, thinking back on it, she wouldn't know which of them moved first, but suddenly she was covering his sex, shaping her fingers to his arousal, cupping the heaviness beneath.

"Chris." He made a deep, choking sound. She started to take her hand away, but he held it fast. "It's okay, okay." He made another sound when he swallowed. "How much longer till we're home?"

Chris looked out the window. It was a minute before she could focus, a minute more before she could identify the street they were on. "Two more blocks." She glanced up at his face, where the tension was marked. A surge of feeling welled up from inside, propelling her mouth to his jaw. She kissed it once, moved an inch, kissed it again. Her voice was like down against his rough skin. "Can you make it?"

"Oh, yeah," he gritted, and released her hand. "Loosen my tie, Chris? I'm being strangled."

She loosened it and unbuttoned the top button. "Better?"

"Yes . . . listen, Chris, if you think there's even the slightest chance that you may get cold feet on me and want to call this off, better tell me now so I can run around the block a couple of times before we go inside." He didn't think they were going to get in much talking or visiting or eating. They'd already passed that point.

"I won't get cold feet," she said, and knew she wouldn't, couldn't. She was too hot.

"What about the food?"

"It'll hold." She took a shallow breath. "Gideon, what I said the other night about birth control? I still don't have anything. I was thinking I should see my doctor, then I didn't know whether we'd really, uh, get together, and I felt funny. Do you have something?"

Turning into her street, he nodded. In a gritty whisper, he said, "Will you help me put it on?"

Her insides grew swollen at the thought. "I don't know how."

"I'll show you."

"So we'll be sharing the responsibility?"

"I wasn't thinking of it that way."

"What were you thinking of?"

"The turn-on. Having you touch me—having you look at me—" He was torturing himself, unable to stop.

"Gideon, what I was trying to tell you before—"

"Jeez, I've never talked about making love this way. Does it sound calculated?" He turned onto the driveway.

"It sounds hot."

"I *feel* hot." He pulled as close to the garage as he could.

"Gideon, there's something I want to *tell* you." She rushed the words out, fearful of being cut off again. "I may have had a baby, but I'm pretty new at this. I haven't even—"

"Shh," he whispered, pressing his fingers to her mouth. Opening the door, he slid out, drawing her along in nearly the same motion. A supportive arm circled her shoulders and hugged her to him as he guided her quickly toward the door. Once inside, with the cold air and all of humanity locked out, he pressed her to the wall, ran his mouth from her forehead, down her nose to her lips. She smelled sweet, almost innocent, and was soft to match. That softness burned into him, from the spot, waist high, where their bodies met to the one at the knee where they parted. She was giving, yielding. Her chin tipped up under the light urging of his thumbs. Her mouth opened to his, welcoming him inside. Every move she made was untutored, purely instinctive, intensely feminine. Each one called to the man in him that craved her possession.

"The nice thing," he breathed against her forehead as he pushed away the shoulders of her coat, "would have been to wait on this until later, but I can't, Chris." The coat slipped to the floor. "If that makes me a not-nice man, I guess that's what I am, but I need you too much now." His fingers met at her throat, touched the collar of her dress and the top buttons, then separated and slid over silk to her breasts. It was the first time he'd touched her there. She was full and firm. Even through her dress and a bra, he could feel the tightness of her nipples.

The sensation of being touched and held was so charged, Chris thought she'd die—just explode. With a small sound, she covered his hands.

He was instantly concerned. As aroused as he was, he had promised to make it good for her, and if it killed him, he intended to do just that. "Hurt?"

"Not enough." She felt impatient and greedy. Transferring her hands from her chest to his, she ran her open palms over him while he worked at the buttons of her dress. When it was open to the waist, she felt him part the fabric, then release the center clasp of her bra. She was holding him at the hips by that time, needing an anchor, feeling momentarily shy when he peeled back the lace and cool air hit her breasts.

Gideon sensed her shyness, and it fueled his fire. In the past, he'd had the most experienced of women, but none sparked him as Chris did. Angling his upper body away, he took pleasure in what he'd unclothed. Her breasts were pale, strawberry at their crests, quivering with each shallow breath she took.

He was smitten. Never in his life had he seen anything as beautiful as Chris against that door with her fingers clutching his hips, her eyes lowered to his belt, her dress open and her breasts bare and waiting. Unable to resist, he ducked his head and put his mouth to one. He drew it in. His tongue raked its turgid tip.

She cried out, a frantic whisper of his name.

"I want you so badly," he moaned. Dragging himself from her breast, he straightened and tore off his blazer. Holding her gaze, which had risen with him, he tugged off his tie, unbuttoned his shirt and unfastened his pants. Then he slid his fingers into her hair, held her head still and took her mouth in a strong, sucking kiss.

Chris wanted more than that. "Upstairs," she gasped when he finally allowed her a breath. "I want you in my bed." She took his hand, but no leading was necessary. He was right beside her, half-running up the stairs, stopping midway for another deep kiss before continuing to the top.

Her room was shadowed, lit only from the hall, though neither of them seemed aware. They were kissing again within seconds, but this time their hands were at work, fumbling with buttons, zippers and sleeves. Their fingers tangled. They alternately laughed, moaned and gasped. She was sitting on the edge of the bed pulling the stockings from her feet when he came down beside her.

"Help me," he said, fiddling with a small foil pack.

For a minute, she couldn't breathe. He was stark naked and fully aroused. She'd known he would be, of course, still her startled eyes were drawn to the thickly thatched spot from which his arousal jutted so tall and straight.

At her utter stillness, Gideon raised his head. He didn't have to follow her gaze to know what she was looking at. The thought that she might be afraid gave him the control he wouldn't otherwise have had. "It won't hurt," he whispered, drawing her close. "You know that. You've done this before."

"But I've never seen it before," she whispered back. "That was what I've been trying to tell you. I have lots of brothers, but by the time they reached puberty, I was out of the house. And with Brant it was always so dark." Tremulously she touched his stomach. "I'm not afraid. You're very beautiful." From his navel, she brushed the back of her fingers down the thin, dark line to where the hair grew more dense, then on to his velvety strength. Satin on steel, it seemed to her. She explored it lightly, felt it flex and grow.

Gideon croaked out her name.

She looked up. "Too much?"

"Too little." He reached again for the foil pack, but no sooner had he removed the condom than she took it from him.

"Tell me how," she whispered.

He told her. With surprising ease, given her trembling and his hardness, she had the condom on. Then, feeling proud and excited and filled with something else that was nearly overwhelming, she slipped her arms around his neck and put her mouth to his. "Love me?"

"I do," he muttered, near the end of his tether. With an arm around her slender waist, he fell over onto the bed, sweeping her beneath him as he drew them both up toward the pillows.

That was when Chris felt the full force of his nakedness. He was man through and through, from the luxury of his weight to the friction of his limbs. His hands seemed everywhere, touching her in large sweeps from her breasts to her hips, then the hot spot between her legs. Suddenly without patience, she opened for him.

"Hurry!"

Taut and trembling, Gideon lifted himself, positioned himself and slowly, slowly sank into the tightest sheath that had ever encased him. "There. Ah. Chris, you're so small."

She felt it. Small, feminine and cherished. And she loved it.

"Am I hurting you?" he asked.

"Oh, no. You feel so new. So special. So big."

Gideon nearly came. He went very still for a minute, shut his eyes tight, gritted his teeth until he'd regained control. "What you do to me."

Chris was thinking the same thing about him, because the small pinching she'd first felt at his entry was gone, leaving only a yearning to be stroked. Grasping his hair, she looked up at him and said, "Make love to me now, Gideon. Do it."

He didn't need any more urging than that. Withdrawing nearly all the way, he surged back with a cry of triumph, then repeated the pattern in a rhythm that seemed to anticipate, then mirror her need. Chris surrendered to that need, letting it take her higher and higher until, closing her eyes and arching her back, she tumbled head-on into a mindless riot of sensation.

Somewhere at the tail end of the riot, a low light came on, but awareness was slow to return. When her breathing had finally slowed and she opened her eyes, she found Gideon propped above her, looking down with a smile. He'd managed to light the lamp beside the bed without leaving her; he was as rigid as ever inside her. But that didn't seem to be bothering him. Though the muscles of his upper arms were taut beneath her hands and his breathing was heavy, something pleased him immensely.

"What?" she whispered with a shy smile.

"You wouldn't ask that if you could see what I do," he replied. His voice was low and husky, as tight as his body, but he wasn't rushing toward his own release. There was too much pleasure to be gained just in looking at Chris, with her blond hair mussed, her cheeks pink, her skin aglow with a light sheen of sweat, her lips rosy and full. There was too much pleasure to be gained just in holding himself inside her, knowing that for a short time she was all his. He felt more loved than he ever had in his life. "Was it good?"

She nodded. "You touch me, and . . . poof!"

His grin broadened. "That's good. I want it like that."

"But you haven't come."

"I will." He took a deep, shuddering breath. "I do love you, y'know."

She felt a burst of heat in the area of her heart. "How can you tell?"

"Because of what I feel, like I could stay this way forever and be perfectly happy. Before, when we were downstairs and then in the car, I thought I'd die if I didn't get into you fast, and maybe I would have. But now that I'm here, there's no rush. What you looked like when you came—what that look did to me—was more satisfying than any climax I've ever had."

Chris felt tears pool in the outside corners of her eyes. "That's beautiful," she whispered. She touched his chest, running a finger by his small, dark nipple. "You're beautiful." Giving more freedom to her hands, she let them familiarize themselves with the wedge of fine hair beneath his collarbone, the muscular ridges of his shoulders, the tapering strength of his back. She was entranced by his perfection, his mix of hard and soft, ragged and smooth, flat and curved. "You *are* beautiful," she whispered again. Curving her hands to his backside, she arched her back and rose off the bed to put her mouth to his throat.

Gideon lost it then. In her slow, gentle way, she was driving him to distraction. Unable to wait any longer, he began to make love to her again. He tempered himself only at the end, when he felt her coming so close, and when her senses erupted for a second time, he gave in to his own powerful release.

Later, much later that night, after the New Year had been welcomed in with toasts and kisses, after Jill and her friends had been fetched and settled, after Gideon had left for the ride back to Worcester and Chris was in bed, she thought about all that had happened.

Gideon had been incredible. He'd made love to her yet another time in her bed, then once in the shower before they dressed. It wasn't the fact of his physical prowess that impressed her as much as the soft things he'd said, the adoring look in his eye and the cherished way he'd made her feel.

Brant had never done that.

More than once, as she lay in bed that night, then on subsequent nights after talking with Gideon on the phone, she wondered if she loved him. The thought was a sobering one. She didn't have faith in herself when it came to love. She'd misjudged once before, and had spent fifteen years trying to make up for it to Jill. If she loved Gideon now, if she became more deeply involved with him than she already was, Jill was bound to be affected. Worse, if the involvement deepened and Jill came to love him, too, and then something happened, Chris would never forgive herself.

The dilemma was whether to take the chance or leave things the way they were. The answer eluded her.

8

Of all the months of the year, Chris liked January the least. It was the coldest and most bleak, physically and emotionally, a necessary evil to be suffered through to reach February, which had a vacation, at least. And then March came with its lengthening days, and April with its promise of rebirth, and by then she had it made.

This year, January was fun. For one thing, she got down to serious work on Crosslyn Rise, poring over Carter's plans, visiting the site at least once a week to check on the progress, wading through swatches of wallpaper and carpeting, studying furniture and cabinetry designs, pondering electrical and bathroom fixtures, and kitchen appliances.

Though she would be working with buyers as they came along later that summer, the plan was to completely outfit a model apartment in one of the units for potential clients to see. Moreover, she would be decorating the entire mansion, once it was subdivided into a restaurant, a health club and a meeting place. For that, she would be calling in experts to help, but she was the coordinator.

There was lots to think about, but she loved it. She also loved spending time with Gideon, which was probably why she went to the Rise so often, given the season and the relatively slow rate of the work. They argued often, but within reason. Though she'd yielded on the issue of winding stairways, she wanted marble tiles in the bathrooms, Corian in the kitchens, and full walls of brick where the fireplaces would go. Invariably Gideon rebelled at the cost, just as inevitably he went out of his way to try to accommodate her. Sometimes he made it, sometimes he didn't. But he tried. She couldn't ask for more.

January was also bright because she saw him after work. She kept it to once a week, on the weekend when Jill might have other plans, but the anticipation of that one night, along with his regular phone calls, kept her feeling alive in ways she hadn't known she'd been missing.

Come February, he asked to stay the weekend at her place, but she was uncomfortable with that. "Jill will be in and out. I just can't."

They were lying face-to-face on a bed in a small motel off the highway not far from Crosslyn Rise. It was three o'clock on a Thursday afternoon. Working together at the Rise shortly before, they'd suffered a sharp desire attack. The motel had been Gideon's suggestion. Chris hadn't protested.

Now, in the afterglow of what had been more hot and exciting than ever, Gideon only knew that he needed more of her. "Jill knows what's going on."

"She doesn't know that we sleep together." They'd been careful about that, choosing their time together with care.

"She knows," he insisted. "She's a perceptive kid. She sees the way we look at each other, the way we touch. She was the one who noticed the hand-holding that first day. You think she doesn't suspect that there's more than hands involved now?"

"I don't know what she suspects," Chris replied, feeling unsettled because it was true. And it was her own fault. She didn't have the courage to ask. "But I think it would be awkward for her if you slept over. It's too soon."

Nothing could be too soon for Gideon, whose love for Chris kept growing. Although he sensed she wasn't really ready, he wanted to ask her to marry him, which was a *really* big step. He'd been footloose and fancy-free for a good long time. But he was willing to give it all up for Chris. He *had* given it all up. Since meeting her, he hadn't dated another woman. Footloose and fancy-free had lost its lure.

He did agree, though, that Jill was a concern. "Does she ask you questions about what we do?"

"Surface ones, like where we ate and what we had for dinner."

"Do you think she accepts me?" He knew that Jill liked him, and remembered all too clearly the permission she'd given him to date Chris. But that had been before he'd started doing it. Faced with the reality of having someone to compete with for her mother's time, she might have had second thoughts.

Chris moved her hand through the hair on his chest. "She accepts you as someone I have a good time with on the weekends."

"But not as my lover?"

"She doesn't know you are."

"You think."

After a minute, she admitted, "I think."

"Maybe you should tell her. You're young. You're healthy. You're an adult. You have every right to want to be with a man."

"I'm supposed to set an example for her."

The sound of that gave Gideon a chill. He drew her closer to ward it off. "You're not doing anything illegal or immoral. You're making love with a man you care deeply about." His voice lowered. "You do care that way, don't you?"

Her eyes were soft, as was her voice. "You know I do." For a minute, secure in his arms, enveloped by his scent and lost in his gaze, she was engulfed by a longing for forever. Then the minute passed and reality returned. "But you have to understand, Gideon. You're the first man I've dated, really dated, in Jill's memory, and we haven't been doing it for long. If I suddenly have you staying the night, she's apt to think that it's okay to do that after a couple of dates."

"It is. Sometimes."

"She's only fifteen!"

"And you're thirty-three. She's bright enough to see the difference. It's okay for you to be doing what we're doing, Chris. It's *right* for you to be doing it, given what you feel. You're a passionate woman." How well he knew. Each time they made love, she was more hungry, more aggressive. "How you kept it locked away for so long is beyond me."

"It wasn't any big thing. I never wanted another man the way I do you."

"Not even Brant?" he couldn't resist asking.

"Not even Brant," she said, and knew it was true. What she felt for Gideon, what she did with him, had nothing to do with growing up, experimenting, feeling her oats or rebelling. It had to do with mature desires and deep inner feelings. "We were young. Too young. I don't want Jill doing what we did."

"You can't put a chastity belt on her."

"No, but I can teach her the importance of waiting."

"Would you have her be a virgin at her wedding?"

"I wouldn't mind it."

"That's unrealistic, Chris."

"I know. But it's not unrealistic to encourage her to wait until someone important to her comes along. I've tried to teach her that lovemaking is special."

"It is. So why can't you tell her that we do it?"

"I can't. She'll jump to conclusions."

"So talk to her. Explain."

But Chris wasn't ready for that. "She's always come first in my life. She may get nervous."

"So you'll talk to her more. You'll explain more. You two are close. You talk about everything else. Why not this?"

She wished she could make him understand. "Because it's so *basic*."

"You're right about that," Gideon drawled, then grew intense. "Lord, Chris, do you know how much I want to sleep with you? Not make love. *Sleep.* Roll over with you tucked up against me. Wake up that way, too."

"And then what would happen?" she asked knowingly.

"We'd make love."

"Right. With Jill in the next room, listening to the headboard bang rhythmically against the wall."

"So we'll pull the bed out."

"The *frame* squeaks."

"I'm a handyman. I'll fix it."

"You're missing the *point*."

"So we won't make love. I'll just go through the rest of the day suffering silently—"

"Gideon," she pleaded softly, "I need time. That's all. I need time to get Jill accustomed to a man in my life. I owe it to her, don't you see?"

As he saw it, she owed things to herself, too. But, then, he'd never been a parent. He'd never felt the kind of responsibility for another human being that Chris felt so keenly for Jill. Loving Chris as he did, he had to respect her feelings.

"Okay," he said in surrender, "then we go to plan B."

"Plan B?"

"We go away together."

Chris was dumbfounded. "Did you hear *anything* I said?"

"All three of us. Jill has school vacation coming up in two weeks. So we'll make reservations and go somewhere together. That way, she'll be able to get used to the idea of our being together."

"But that'll be no different than having you over at the house! The same problem exists."

"Not if we book separate rooms." When Chris seemed to listen at that, he went on. "You and Jill room together. I'll have my own. We could either go north to ski or south to sun and swim."

Chris wanted to tell him he was crazy, except that idea wasn't bad. In fact, the more she thought of it, the more she liked it. "Do you ski?" she asked.

"Sure, I ski," he answered. "I mean, I may not do my turns as neatly as I do my lay-ups, but neither do I make a fool out of myself." He could see she was tempted. "Ever been to Stowe?"

She shook her head against his shoulder. "Only to Woodstock, and not for skiing. Stowe is farther north. I never wanted to drive that long."

"Would you want to with me?"

"I wouldn't mind it."

"What about Jill?"

"She'd be game. She's dying to go skiing."

"Does she know how?"

"Barely."

"No sweat. The instructors are good. Would you prefer a condo or an inn?"

"An inn."

"Separate rooms?"

She nodded.

"Would you visit me in mine?"

She grinned. "Maybe."

With a grin of his own, he slid an arm around her hips, which was where, by a stretch of the imagination, there was a touch of fullness. "Maybe?"

"If it isn't too hard."

"It'll definitely be hard."

"Is that a warning," she asked softly, "or a promise?"

Eyes smoldering, he rolled to his back and drew her on top. His large hands cupped her head, directing her down for his kiss. It was the only answer he gave.

When Chris told Jill that they were going skiing, her eyes lit up. When she told her that Gideon would be coming, the light faded a little. "I didn't know he skied," she said with reluctant interest.

"I didn't, either. But he does. And he's been to Stowe before, so he knows the good places to eat."

"Will we rent a condo?"

"I thought we'd go to an inn." She paused. "I thought you'd be more comfortable that way."

"Will I have my own room?"

"We'll share, you and me."

Jill seemed surprised by that, and relieved. "You're not rooming with Gideon?"

Chris shook her head. "I'm rooming with you."

"Won't he mind?"

"He knows that's the way it has to be."

Jill considered that. "Do you wish it was different?"

"In what sense?"

"That you two were going away alone?"

"Of course not. You're my best friend."

"And what's he?"

"He's a man I'm seeing, who I like a lot."

"Do you love him?"

"You've asked me that before. What did I tell you then?"

"That it was too soon to ask you, but you've seen him a lot since then. You must have some idea what you feel. Or what you think you can feel. If we're going skiing with him—"

"We're doing it because it sounds like fun."

"We could drive up there, you and me, just ourselves."

"But it was Gideon's idea." She gave Jill a funny look. "Weren't you the one who felt so badly that he had to spend Christmas all by himself in a lonely house?"

"Yeah, but this is different. This is purely voluntary. It's my vacation time. Not his."

Chris felt a stab of concern. "Would you rather he not go?"

"No. He can go."

"Such enthusiasm," she teased, trying to hide her unease. "I thought you liked him."

"I *do*. And I'm *glad* we're going skiing with him. I just want to know if you love him."

Chris thought about it for a minute before finally, truthfully, saying, "I don't know. There are times when I think I do, but then there are so many considerations—''

"Like what?"

"Like whether he's prepared to play second fiddle to you. You come first, Jill. You always have and always will."

"But that's not fair to you. Maybe you want to be with Gideon. Maybe you *should* be with him."

"How would you feel if I were?"

Jill was awhile in answering. The words were cautious when they came. "Happy for you. Happy for Gideon."

"And for you?"

"Happy, too, I guess."

"You don't sound convinced."

She looked at her hands. "I don't know. It just takes some getting used to. I mean, I'd really like it because then you'd have things to do, yourself, and I wouldn't feel badly leaving you home all alone."

Chris hadn't realized. "Do you do that?"

"Sometimes. But then I like knowing you're here. I like knowing you're waiting for me. Selfish, huh?"

Brushing a wisp of dark hair from Jill's cheek, Chris said, "Not selfish at all. Just a little worried. You've been used to one thing, and now you see the possibility of things changing. Don't you think the idea of change frightens me, too? Don't you think it comes into play when you ask if I love Gideon?"

"Does it?"

"Sure, it does. I'm used to my life, our life. I like it. I'm not sure I want anything to disturb it."

"But if you love Gideon—"

"I don't know for sure that I do, which is one of the reasons why I really want the three of us to go on this trip. If I'm going to love any man, you'll have to feel comfortable with him—and vice versa—because no matter what else happens, I'm your mother. Always. I'll be here for you even if I love *ten* guys."

Jill smirked. "Ten guys? Fat chance. You're such a prude."

"What is that supposed to mean?" Chris asked with an indignance that was only half-feigned.

"You haven't even gone to bed with Gideon! I mean, look at him. He's gorgeous. Jenny and Laura are *still* drooling over him. Why aren't you?"

"Why aren't I drooling?"

"Why aren't you sleeping with him?"

Chris swallowed. As openings went, it was perfect. Remembering the conversation she'd had such a short time before with Gideon, she knew he was right. She and Jill were close. She'd always prided herself on forthrightness. She could explain her feelings. They could talk. It was time.

"How do you know I'm not?" she asked gently.

While Jill didn't jump immediately at the suggestion, she grew more alert. "When do you have time?"

"You make time for what you want."

"I mean, when have you had the *chance*?"

"You find chances, if you want them."

Jill was quiet. After a minute, she blurted out, "So have you—or haven't you?"

"Is it important to you to know?"

She backed down. "Not if you don't want to tell me."

"I do. I want to tell you. I want to, because some of the things Gideon and I have shared have been very, very beautiful. I've always told you that. With the right person, making love is precious."

Jill seemed suddenly shy, as though this Chris was a new and different person from the one she'd known moments before. "So you have," she whispered.

Chris nodded. "He is . . . very special."

"Does he love you?"

"Yes."

"Do you think you'll marry him?"

Chris had taught her that lovemaking should be with someone special, that marriage should be with someone special. So Jill had made the connection, as the mother in Chris wanted her to. Now Chris was caught in the middle.

"I don't know, honey. If what I feel for him proves to be love, I might. But that would be a long way off."

"Why?"

"Because I wouldn't do anything until you went to college."

"Will a man like Gideon wait around that long?"

"If he loves me enough. Maybe that's the test."

"What if you get pregnant before that?"

"Pregnant. Jill, I've taught *you* about using birth control. Don't you think I practice it myself?" She'd seen her doctor right after New Year's.

"What do you use?"

"*Jill.*"

"I'm not supposed to ask that?"

Chris closed her eyes for a second, then reached for her daughter's hand. "Of course you can. This is new for me. That's all."

"Birth control is?"

"Telling you about *my* using it is."

"Wouldn't you want to know what I used?"

"Jill, you're not—"

"No! But if I were, wouldn't you want me to discuss it with you?"

"Definitely."

"So?"

Chris sighed. "I got a diaphragm."

"Do you like it?"

"Uh, well, uh, it's okay, I mean, it's safe and effective, and if you, uh, if you have to use something—"

Jill started to laugh.

"What's so funny?"

"You. You're all red."

"This is *embarrassing*."

"Why? You've told me so many other things without getting embarrassed."

"This is different." She searched for the words. "It's like you're my mother, but I've never had this kind of discussion with my mother."

"That's why I came along."

"And the very best thing you were. I've never, *never* regretted having you, though there are times when I wished my timing had been better. There are times when I wish I could have given you a family of your own, maybe brothers and sisters."

"You could have more babies."

"Hey, I just said I was using birth control."

"But you could stop. Any time you wanted to. You're young enough to have lots more kids. Does Gideon want them?"

"I don't know. We haven't gotten that far."

"Do you?"

"I don't know. You'd be a pretty hard act to follow."

"Naturally," Jill said with a grin.

Chris grinned right back. "Naturally." She took a breath. "So. What do you say? Want to go skiing?"

The inn was small and quaint, with six guest rooms on the second floor and two baths. If she'd wanted to be secretive, Chris would have stolen into Gideon's room, which was down the hall from hers and Jill's, when she was supposedly using the bathroom. But Jill would have known. Besides, she wanted more time.

So she and Gideon returned to his room shortly after Jill had joined an afternoon ski class. Knowing that it would be three hours before she was done, they felt they had all the time in the world.

Chris never failed to marvel at Gideon's body, and this time was no exception. Wearing ski garb—navy stretch pants that clung to him like static and a lime-green turtleneck sweater that matched his navy-and-green parka—he presented the kind of figure that was regularly photographed for the pages of *W*. When that garb came off, though, slowly revealing broad shoulders, a lean stomach and long, long legs, he was Chris's own very personal fantasy come to life.

Dropping her panties onto the floor by the rest of her things, she approached him. Her hands found his shoulders, then moved down and around and back. "When we're out on the slopes," she said in a sultry whisper, "women do double takes when you pass. Your moves may not be studied, but you have a natural grace." She moved closer, bringing her breasts, her belly, her thighs into contact with his. "You do this way, too," she said. Opening her mouth on his neck, she dragged her lips over that corded column. "You are an incredible male." Her palms chafed his thighs, moving slowly in to frame his sex.

Gideon was sure he'd died and gone to heaven. "You make me this way," he said. "It's all for you." Lowering his head, he caught her lips at the same time that he lifted her legs to his hips. He slid into her with the comfort and ease of an old lover and the excitement of a new one.

Familiarity gave them the confidence to be inventive, and a boundless hunger gave them the fuel. Gideon loved her standing up, then sitting on the edge of the bed, then, with Chris astride, on the sheets. He paused midway to love her with his tongue until she was wild with need, then shot back into her with a speed and force that she welcomed. The quiet in the room was broken by gasps and cries. By the time those finally eased, they were both sated, their bodies slick with sweat, tangled but limp.

"Marry me, Chris."

She was half-asleep. "Hmm?"

"I want to marry you."

"I know," she mumbled.

"Will you?"

Eyes closed, she kissed the smooth, soft spot just before his armpit. "Ask me later. Can't think now."

Gideon gave her ten minutes. Then he nudged her partly awake, tipped up her face with a finger and kissed her the rest of the way.

She grinned. "Hi."

"Hi, yourself." He looked at her, then looked some more. Never in a million years would he tire of seeing her after they made love, when she was warm and wet and sensual. He had never before had the stamina to make love three or four times in a night, but he had it with Chris. She inspired him to great heights. "Are you up?"

Sleepily she nodded. "This is so nice. I'm *so* glad we came here."

"Me, too." He paused, figuring he'd take a different, less direct tack this time. "Hard to believe the week's almost done. I could take this on a regular basis for the next thirty or forty years."

Even in her half-dreamy state, Chris knew what he meant. "There's something about ski country. The air is so clear. So cold. So invigorating. It's so warm coming inside."

"When I grow up," Gideon said, "I'm going to buy a place, maybe not as far north as this, but closer, so I can use it on weekends." He ran the pad of his thumb over her eyebrows, first one, then the other. "What do you think? Make any sense?"

Chris thought the idea sounded divine. "What kind of place?" she asked, dreaming wide awake now.

"Something old. With charm."

"A Victorian on the edge of a town green, with the white spire of a church at one end and the stone chimney of the local library at the other."

"You got it. I'd do the place over inside myself, so that it had every modern convenience. I'd break down walls so everything was open, and redo the fireplace so you could see the fire front and back. I'd put in lofts and skylights and spiral stairways and—"

"A Jacuzzi."

"You'd like one?"

"Definitely."

"We've never made love in a Jacuzzi."

"I know." Chris let herself imagine it. "I'd like to."

He was getting hard just thinking of it. "So would I."

"You should have put one in when you built your house."

"But I hadn't met you then. Real men don't soak in tubs unless there's a woman with them, and you're the only woman I've ever entertained at my house."

"The only one?"

"Only one. I love you."

She smiled helplessly. "I know."

"How 'bout you?"

"I'm workin' on it," she teased.

But he was serious. "How far have you come?"

"I'm at the point," she said, "of being happier with you than I've ever been before in my life." There were times when she felt delirious inside, so pleased and excited that she didn't know what to do with her excess energy.

"How far is that from being in love?"

"Pretty close, I guess."

"How long will it take to make 'pretty close' *there*?"

"I don't know." That was where things got hairy, because she knew what was coming next.

"I need you, Chris," he said in the slow, rumbling voice that she'd come to associate with Gideon at his most intense. "I want to be with you morning and night for the rest of my life. I want us to get married."

She'd heard him ask her before, of course, but in the afterglow of loving, she'd pushed it from her mind. She couldn't do that now. She looked up at him to answer, then was momentarily stunned by the look in his eyes. They were so filled with love—and desperation—that she had to fight for a breath.

Coming up over him, she kissed him softly. Her forearms, resting on his chest, held her in position to meet his gaze. "I never thought I'd say this, I really didn't, because marriage wasn't something I ever spent much time considering, but I could almost see myself marrying you, Gideon. I could. I feel so much for you that it overwhelms me sometimes."

"That's love."

"Maybe. But I have to be sure. For me, and for you, and for Jill. I have to know it'll last."

"It'll last."

"So says every couple when they exchange wedding vows, but look at the statistics. I thought I was in love once, and I wasn't."

"You were too young to know what love was about. You're older now."

"We're both older. Look at you. You're almost forty. You were married once, and it didn't work, and now you've been single for years. Is what you feel for me different from what you felt for your first wife?"

"Totally," he said with conviction. "I never wanted to spend all my time with her, not even at the beginning. She had a limited time and place in my life. I had my friends, my business, my games, and I didn't want her to have any part of them. With you, I'm passing up all those other things just to be with you."

"You shouldn't—"

"I *want* to. I'd much *rather* be with you than be with anyone else. I'd much rather be with you than be alone. My first marriage wasn't fun. Being with you is. Know what I want?" The look in his eyes was precious in its enthusiasm.

"What?"

"I want us to work together all the time. We'd be partners. I build, you decorate. Would you like that?"

She would, a whole lot, but her throat was so tight that she could only nod her answer.

He ran his finger over her lips. "I want to make you happy, Chris, and that's another thing that's different from the first time. I never thought about making Julie happy. I was almost defiant about going on with my life as though marriage didn't change it at all." He made a small sound. "I'm not even married to you yet, and my life has changed. Everything I do is geared to when I'll be seeing you again, and I love it that way." He gave her a lopsided grin. "Johnny thinks I'm sick. We were having a sandwich at the diner the other day and these two women came in. Ten, fifteen, twenty minutes went by and he started looking at me strangely."

"Why?"

"Because he thought they were real lookers and I wasn't even interested. I guess they were pretty, but that's all. Hell, I don't even wink at Cookie anymore!"

"Poor Cookie."

"Yeah, she was kinda hurt."

"You have my permission to wink. There's no harm in that."

"But winking is a kind of come-on. It's like me saying, 'I'm a man, and I think you're cute.' But I'm not thinking about anyone else being cute anymore. No one but you."

"Oh, Gideon."

"I've even thought about living arrangements. We could buy a piece of land halfway between Worcester and Belmont, something really pretty, big and wooded. There're lots of bedroom communities with good schools for Jill—"

"I can't change her."

"Why not?"

"Because she's in high school. She's with friends she's grown up with, and they're just getting to the fun years. It'd be cruel to take her away from that."

"Then we'll live in Belmont until she's done with high school, and in the meanwhile we can be building our dream house—"

She pressed a hand to his mouth. "Shh."

"What?"

"You're being too accommodating."

"That's the point. I love you, so I *want* to be accommodating."

"But I can't be accommodating back!" she cried. "Don't you see? You're right about love meaning that, but I'm not free to love that way. I have Jill. I want things to be so right for her in the next few years."

Gideon felt that they had circled around and were right back to the point where they'd been weeks before. It was frustrating, but he wasn't about to give up. "I want things right for her, too. My coming into your life doesn't have to change anything."

"But it will. It will. And then if something goes wrong—"

"What something?"

"With our relationship, and there'd be tension and upset. I don't want to subject Jill to that. She's been so good about not having a father."

"But that's *another* thing," he went on. "You could *give* her a father, if you wanted. Me."

"It's not the same."

Gideon let the words sink in, along with the look on Chris's face. The moment was enlightening. "You feel guilty about that, don't you?"

"Yes, I feel guilty."

Wrapping his arms around her, he hugged her. "After all you've given Jill, the last thing you should be feeling is guilty. My God, Chris, you've been a saint."

"Not quite," she murmured, though she liked hearing him say it.

"Jill has had more love than most kids with *two* parents get. She wouldn't be as well adjusted if that weren't so."

"I want her to stay well adjusted."

"So do I," he said, and let it go at that. He knew from experience that where Jill's welfare was concerned, Chris was unyielding. It was simply going to be up to him, over the next weeks and months, to show her that he'd be good for Jill, too.

9

Gideon had the best of intentions. When he took Chris to a movie, he suggested Jill bring a friend along. When a foot of snow fell and school was canceled, he drove in from Worcester with a toboggan and took them all sliding. When Jill wanted to buy a gift for Chris's birthday, he took her to not one mall, not two, but *three* before she found what she wanted. And he was thrilled to do it. He genuinely enjoyed Jill. And he thought she enjoyed him.

Chris did, too. Jill looked forward to seeing him. At other times, though, she was more quiet than usual. More than once, when she was at the kitchen table doing homework at night and Chris was nearby, talking softly on the phone to Gideon, she sensed Jill looking at her, sensed a pensiveness that had nothing to do with schoolwork. At times, she thought that pensiveness was brooding, but when she asked, Jill shook her head in denial.

March came, then April, and Chris began to worry in earnest. Jill just wasn't herself. She was doing fine in school, and her social life was as active as ever, but at home she was definitely distracted. She continued to deny there was a problem, and Chris could only push so far. She thought, though, that it might be wise for them to spend some time alone together. They hadn't done it much of late, what with Chris's work—she was up to her ears with orders both for the model condo at Crosslyn Rise and the mansion, itself—and Gideon's presence. So, over dinner at home one mid-week night, she broached the topic.

"Any thoughts on vacation, Jill?" When Jill set down her fork, alert but silent, Chris said, "I was thinking that we could go down to New York for a few days."

"New York?"

"Uh-huh. Just the two of us. We could shop, eat out, maybe take in a show or two. Would you like that?"

Jill lifted her fork again and pushed a piece of chicken around the plate.

"Jill?"

The fork settled. Looking young and vulnerable, Jill met her gaze. "I was thinking I'd use that vacation for something else."

"What's that?"

"I want to meet my father."

Chris felt the blood leave her face. Of all the things she'd imagined Jill wanting to do, that wasn't one. "Your father?"

"He's out there. I want to meet him."

"Uh, uh, what—" she cleared her throat "—what brought this on?"

Jill shrugged. "I'm curious."

"Is this what's been getting you down lately?"

"Not getting me down. But I've been thinking about it a lot. I really want to know who he is. I want to see him."

Chris felt dizzy. She took a deep breath to steady herself. "Uh, honey, I don't know where he is."

"You said he was in Arizona," Jill shot back in an accusing tone.

Chris tried to be conciliatory. "He was, last time I heard, but that was second- or thirdhand, and years ago."

"Where in Arizona?"

"Phoenix."

"So I could start looking there."

"In *person*?"

"Of course not. I'd call Directory Assistance. How many Brant Conways can there be?"

"Lots."

"Okay. You said he sells real estate. There must be some state list of people who do that. If he was there even ten years ago, he must have worked with someone who's kept in touch with him. I could find all that out on the phone."

Chris realized that Jill had given the possibilities a certain amount of very adult thought. She wondered how far that adult thought had gone. "And then what?"

"Then I'll call him, then fly out to see him during vacation."

"What if he doesn't want that?"

"Then we'll arrange another time to meet."

"What if he doesn't want that, either?"

"Then we'll arrange something else. There has to be *some* way we can get together."

Chris studied the napkin she was clutching so tightly in her lap. "Has it occurred to you that he might not want to see you?"

Sounding defiant but subdued, Jill said, "Yes. And if he doesn't, I won't go."

"But you'll be hurt in the process. I don't want that, Jill. I've tried to protect you from hurt. You don't *need* Brant. Trust me. You have everything that's good for you here, without him."

"But he's my father."

"Biologically, yes. Beyond that, he's nothing to you."

"He may be a very nice man."

"He may be, but he has his own life and you have yours."

"I don't want to be *in* his life. I just want to *meet* him."

Chris had always recognized the possibility of that, but she had kept it a very distant thought. Suddenly it was real and near, and she wasn't prepared to handle it.

She felt betrayed. She knew it was wrong. But that was how she felt.

"Why now?" she asked, half to herself.

"I already told you that."

But she had a sudden, awful suspicion. "It has something to do with Gideon, doesn't it?"

"What could it have to do with him?"

"He's the first man I've been interested in. In the past few weeks, he's probably come as close as you've ever come to having a father around." She'd known it. Damn it, she'd *known* something would happen. "I'm right, aren't I?"

"I like Gideon. I like being with him."

"But he's made you think of your father."

"It's not *Gideon's* fault."

But Chris had known. She'd *known*. Bolting from the table, she started pacing the room. "I told him it was too much, too fast. I asked him to slow things down, but did he? No. *He* knew what was best."

"Mom—"

"Over and over, I asked him to be patient. I told him I didn't want anything upsetting you. I told you you needed time."

"Mom—"

"The big expert, sticking his nose into other people's business."

"Mom." She was twisted around in her chair. When Chris looked at her, she said, "This is *not Gideon's fault*! I love Gideon. He loves you, and you love him."

"I don't—"

"You do! I see it every night. It's written all over your face when you talk to him on the phone. And I think it's great. I *want* you to love him. I *want* you to marry him. I think it'd be fun to be a family. That's something I could never have with my father, and I accept that. I don't want anything with him. I like what I have. I just want to meet the man, so that I'll know who he is and who I am. Then I can be a step-daughter to Gideon.''

There had been certain times over the years when Chris had found motherhood to be overwhelmingly emotional. One had been when she'd first been presented her gooey, scrunched-up baby girl, another when Jill had gone off on the school bus for the very first time, another when Jill had had the lead in the middle school's musical production of *Snow White and the Seven Dwarfs*. Intense pride always affected Chris.

Intense pride was what she felt at that moment, along with a bit of humility. Fighting back tears, she put her arm around Jill and gave her a tight hug. "You are incredible.''

Jill hugged her back. "I do love you, Mom. I'll always love you. I don't think I could ever love *him*, but I want to know who he is.''

Regaining a modicum of composure, Chris slid back into her chair. She wanted to think clearly, wanted Jill to do the same. "I don't really know much about him. If he has a slew of other children, how will you feel?''

"Okay.''

"What if he's big and bald and fat?''

"Haven't you been the one to always tell me not to judge a book by its cover?''

"But this is your father. You may be fantasizing that he's some kind of god—''

"If he were that, he'd have come for me, not the other way around.'' She took a breath, seeming strong now that she'd aired what had clearly been weighing so heavily on her mind. "Mom, I'm not looking for someone to take your place, and I'm *not* looking for another place to live. I just want to meet my father. Once I've seen him, I'll know who he is and that he exists, and that he knows *I* exist. Then I can go on with my life."

The words were all correct. They were grown-up and sensible. Chris knew that, but the knowledge was small solace for the fear she felt. Jill had been her whole life, and vice versa, for so long, that the thought of Brant intruding in any way was upsetting. She sensed that, for the first time, there was a crack in her relationship with Jill—not a crack as in hostility, but one as in growing up and separating. That too was inevitable, but Chris wasn't ready for it.

Nor was she ready for Gideon when he called that night. "I'm really tired. Why don't we connect later in the week."

He was immediately concerned. "Aren't you feeling well?"

"I'm fine. Just tired."

When he called the next night, she didn't claim fatigue, but she was quiet, answering his questions as briefly as possible, not offering anything extra. "Is something wrong?" he finally asked after five minutes of trying to pull her usual enthusiasm from her.

"Of course not. What could be wrong?"

He didn't know. But he knew she wasn't herself, and he feared that what was upsetting her had to do with him. "You sound angry."

"Not angry. Just busy."

"At ten o'clock at night?"

"I'm trying to get some papers in order. I have a slew of deliveries coming for five different jobs, and if the invoices get messed up—"

"I thought Margie took care of paperwork like that."

"Margie isn't involved the way I am, and I want these things to be right. If there are screwups, I'll have to be cleaning them up at the same time that Crosslyn Rise is picking up—"

Gideon interrupted. "Chris, why are you working so hard?"

"Because I'm a professional. I have commitments."

"But you don't have to work *this* hard."

"I have bills to pay," she snapped. "In case you've forgotten, I have a teenage daughter to support."

"I haven't forgotten," Gideon said quietly. "I want to help you do that."

"You've done enough!"

A heavy silence stretched between them before he said, "What's that supposed to mean?"

"Nothing."

"*What*, Chris?"

She sighed and rubbed the back of her neck. "*Nothing*. Listen, I'm tired and short-tempered. You'd probably be best to avoid me for a little while."

He didn't like the sound of that at all. "A little while?"

"A few days."

"No way. We have a date for dinner tomorrow night."

"Look, maybe that's not such a good idea."

"I think it is." He paused. "You're angry. What have I done? Damn it, Chris, if you don't tell me, I won't know and I can't do a goddamned thing about remedying it. Come on. *Talk* to me."

"Not tonight," she said firmly. "I'll be back in the office sometime after three tomorrow. Call me then and we'll decide what to do about dinner."

Gideon didn't call. True to form, he was there, waiting in her office when she returned. She stopped at the door when she saw him, feeling an overwhelming rush of sensation. He could arouse that, whether she was annoyed with him or not, and it wasn't only physical. Her heart swelled at the sight of him, which was probably why she hadn't wanted to see him. Looking at him, feeling the warm embrace of his eyes and the love that was so clearly behind it, she was more confused than ever about the anger she felt.

"Hi, doll," he said with a gentle smile. He went to her and kissed her cheek, then leaned back. "Uh-oh. I'm still in the doghouse?"

She slipped past him to her desk, where she deposited her briefcase and the folders she carried.

"Chris." He drew her name out in a way that said he knew something was wrong and wanted to know what it was before he lost his patience.

Knowing that she wouldn't have a chance of keeping still with him right there—and realizing she didn't *want* to—she sat down at her desk, linked her hands tightly in her lap, and said, "Jill wants to contact her father."

Gideon hadn't been expecting that, but he wasn't surprised. "Ahh. And that upsets you."

To put it mildly. "Of course, it upsets me! She wants to go off and find a man who, for all intents and purposes, doesn't want her around."

"How do you know that?"

"Because she's fifteen, and he's never once made the slightest attempt to see her—" she held up both hands "—and that's okay by me, because she doesn't need him in her life, but she's suddenly decided that she wants to know who he is. She's going to be hurt. I know it." Her fingers knotted again. "*That's* what I don't want!"

Knowing Chris the way he did, knowing what she wanted in life for Jill, Gideon could understand why she was upset, though he didn't completely agree. "She doesn't have to be hurt. He may be cordial. He may even welcome her."

Chris felt deep, dark fears rush to the surface. "And if that happens, she may want to see him again and again, and that'll mess her up completely."

"Her, or you?"

"What?"

"Are you afraid for her," Gideon repeated patiently, "or for you?"

Chris was furious that he was so calm when she felt as if the bottom of her world were falling away. "For *me*?" Emotional stress brought her out of her chair. "You think I'm being selfish?"

"No, that's not—"

"How *dare* you suggest that!" she fumed. "I've spent the better half of my life doing and thinking and feeling for that child. I've sacrificed a whole lot, and I'd do the same thing again in a minute." Trembling, she steadied her fingertips on the chrome rim of her desk. "Selfish? Who in the *hell* are you to tell me I'm selfish? You've never sacrificed for a child. You've never sacrificed for anyone!"

Gideon was on the verge of coming to his own defense, when Chris raced on. She needed to air what she was feeling, he realized. He also realized that he wanted to know it all. He'd been a nervous wreck wondering what was wrong with her. So, much as it hurt him, he leaned back against the wall, arms folded on his chest, and listened.

"You've lived life for your own pleasure and enjoyment," she charged. "You wanted something, you took it, and that included me. But that wasn't enough, was it? It wasn't enough that we started dating, even though I didn't want to, or that we kept *on* dating, even though I didn't want to, or that we started sleeping together. That wasn't enough for you. You wanted marriage, and you wanted it fast. When I said I was worried about Jill, you said, 'No sweat, she loves me,' and maybe she does. But it's thinking about you and wondering about us and whether we're getting married that's now making her think about Brant!''

Gideon remained quiet, waiting. When she didn't say anything, simply glared at him—albeit with tears in her eyes now, and that tore through him—he said, ''Are you done?''

''If it hadn't been for you, pushing your way into our lives, it wouldn't have *occurred* to her to think of him!''

Again Gideon was quiet, though it was harder to remain so with each word she said. In the old days, he wouldn't have put up with a woman throwing unjust claims at him. He'd either have thrown them right back or walked out the door. So maybe he was sacrificing for Chris now. If so, he was more than happy to do it.

''Can I speak?'' he asked, but again his quiet words spurred her on.

''Everything was so good! We had our lives together, she was well adjusted and happy, not going for alcohol or drugs the way some of the kids at her school are, I was beginning to earn some real money. Then you came along—'' she caught her breath, a single trickle of tears escaping from each eye ''—then you came along and upset it all!''

It was the trickle of tears that did it. Unable to stand still any longer, he left the wall and went to her. ''Honey, I think you're confusing the issues,'' he said softly, but when he reached for her, she batted his hands away.

"I'm not! I've done nothing but go over and over every single aspect of this for the past two days."

"You've lost perspective."

"I have *not*!"

"Maybe if you'd shared it sooner, you would have seen—"

"Seen what?" she cut in shakily. "That you're the answer to my problems? That all I have to do is marry you and let you take me away from here, so Jill can find herself with her father?"

"Of course not!" Gideon argued. "Jill is part of our lives. It's you, me and her. It has been right from the start."

"But it's *not* her," Chris cried, and her chin began to wobble. "She's going off to Arizona to see Brant." Her breathing grew choppy. "Things won't ever be the same again!"

Gideon had had enough. He pulled her into his arms, then held her tighter when she struggled. Within seconds, she went limp against him, and within seconds of that, clutching his sweater, she began to cry softly.

"Oh, baby," he said, crushed by the sound of her sobs. He stroked her blond hair, rubbed her slender back, held her as close as he could until her weeping began to abate. Then he sat against the edge of the desk and propped her between his thighs. Her head was still down, her cheek against his chest. Quietly he began to speak.

"You're right, Chris. Things won't ever be the same again. We've found each other, Jill's growing up,

Crosslyn Rise has been gutted. That's growth. It's progress. And you're afraid, because for the first time in a long time things are changing in your life, and that makes you nervous. It would make me nervous, too, I suppose, but that's just a guess, because you're right, I haven't been in your shoes. I haven't had a child. I haven't raised that child and poured every bit of myself into it. So I don't know what it's really like when suddenly something appears to threaten that relationship."

"I'm so scared," Chris whimpered.

He tightened his arms around her. "I know, baby, I know, but there are a couple of things you're not taking into consideration. First off, just because Jill wants to see Brant, that doesn't mean she'll have an ongoing relationship with him."

"She will. I know she will."

"How do you know?" he challenged. When she didn't answer, he gentled his voice again. "You don't know, because you don't know who Brant is now, and because you're underestimating Jill. She wouldn't do anything to hurt you."

"She wants to see him!"

"She *needs* to see him. It's part of growing up. It's part of forming her identity. She's been wondering about him for a long time, now she needs to finally see who he is, so that she can put the wondering aside and go on living."

The thoughts sounded strangely familiar. In a slow, suspicious voice, Chris asked, "Did you discuss this with her?'' The idea that Jill would go to Gideon before she went to her own mother was cutting.

But Gideon was quick to deny it. ''Are you kidding? She wouldn't open to me that way. At least, not yet.''

''But she said nearly the same thing you just did.''

''That's because it's what she's feeling.''

Chris looked up. ''How would you know what she's feeling?''

He brushed at tear tracks with the pads of his thumbs. ''Because I felt those same things myself when I was a kid. I was younger than she is. I didn't understand it the way she probably does, but after the fact I could see it. My mother came to visit me when I was little, but it wasn't the same. I couldn't put her in any kind of context. I reached a point of wanting—no, *needing*—to go to her, to see where she lived and who she lived with.'' He arched a dark brow. ''You think my dad was pleased? He was *furious*! Couldn't understand why I'd spend all that money to fly all the way across the country to see a woman who hadn't cared enough to hang around. He yelled and yelled and carried on for a good long time until it finally hit me that he was jealous.''

''I'm not jealous,'' Chris claimed, but more quietly. Her mind had been so muddled since Jill had mentioned Brant that she hadn't realized—hadn't remembered—that Gideon had been in a situation not unlike the one Jill was in. ''I'm just scared.''

''Well, my dad was, too. He was scared that I'd take a look at her life and reject him the way she had. He was scared that I'd pick up and move out to California to live with her, and that he'd be left all alone. He didn't even have family, the way you do."

Needing the cushion, she returned her head to his chest. "That doesn't make it any easier."

"I know," he crooned against her hair, "I know. The loss of a child like that would be traumatic in any case. But the fact was that he didn't lose me. I saw where my mother lived, and sure, she had plenty of money and could have given me a hell of a lot if I'd gone out there to live with her, but the fact is that I wouldn't have traded my father's love for a penny of her money in a million years."

It was a minute before his words penetrated fully and sank deep into her soul. Moaning, she slipped her arms around his waist. He was so dear.

But he wasn't done talking. "Don't you think Jill knows what a good thing she has in you? Don't you think she knows how much she loves you?"

"Yes, but she doesn't know how much I love *her*. She doesn't know that I'd be destroyed if she ever decided to live with Brant. He was so horrible doing what he did to me—and to her. One part of me is absolutely infuriated that she even wants to *see* him."

His breath was warm against her forehead. "But you can't tell her that—or show her, because that's not the way you are—so you took your anger out on me. And that's okay, Chris. I'd rather you took it out on me than on her. But you owed me an explanation, at least. It's not fair to refuse to talk to me, like you've done for two nights on the phone. If you want to scream and yell at me, fine. That's what I'm here for. Screaming and yelling is sometimes the only way to get anger out of your system. Or fear. Or worry." His voice grew more fierce. "Just don't shut me out, damn it. Don't shut me out."

Slipping her arms higher on his back, Chris buried her face against his neck. "I'm sorry," she whispered. "I guess you were the only scapegoat around. I've just been so miserable since she brought it up. I keep thinking of all the possibilities—"

"Not all of them. Only the worst ones."

He was probably right, she knew. "I keep thinking that she'll find him and like him and want to stay, or that she'll hate him but he'll like her and want a part of her, even, God forbid, sue for visitation rights. I keep worrying that her going after Brant will open a whole can of worms. She's such a terrific kid. I don't want her messed up."

"She won't be messed up."

Chris raised her eyes to his. "Look at all the kids whose parents are divorced."

"What about them?"

"They're messed up."

"Not all of them. But your situation isn't the same."

"If there's suddenly a tug-of-war between Brant and me, it's the same."

"There won't be any tug-of-war. Jill won't want to live with him. She's happy here, with you and all the friends she's grown up with. You said that yourself when I suggested we build a house somewhere other than Belmont, and it made sense. She isn't about to want to pick up and relocate all of a sudden.''

"What if Brant wants it?"

"He won't want it. Not at this late date."

"But what if he does?"

"You'll tell him no."

"What if he fights?"

"You mean, goes to court? He won't do that." He snorted. "Talk about cans of worms. If he goes to court, you can sue him for back child support. Think he'll pay up?"

"What if he does? What if he does, and then wants visitation rights?"

"He won't have much of a chance of getting them. He knew he had a child fifteen years ago. He chose to ignore her. He didn't give money, and he didn't give time. No court is going to feel terribly sympathetic toward him. Besides, Jill isn't a baby. She's old enough to express her feelings and to have them taken into account."

"In court. Oh, God. I don't want her dragged through anything like that."

"She *won't* be." He took her face in his hands and put conviction into his words. "The chances of anything like that happening are so remote that it's absurd to even be thinking of it now."

"It's not absurd to me. I'm her mother. I *care*."

"So do I, Chris," he stated fiercely, "but it won't do her any good if you're a basket case worrying about worst-case scenarios. Chances are she'll meet the man, and that'll be it."

For the first time, hearing his words and the confidence behind them, Chris let herself believe it might be true. "I'd give anything for that."

He kissed her nose. "She's a good, sensible young woman, her mother's daughter all the way. My guess is that if she ever knew how upset you've been, she'd cancel her plans."

"If she did that, she'd always wonder."

"Uh-huh."

Though she could have done without his agreement, she felt herself beginning to relax. The breath she took was only slightly shaky, a vague reminder of her recent crying jag. "You don't think I'll lose her?"

"No *way* could you lose her. She'll probably go see Brant and then come back and be her good old self." He frowned. "You say the guy's in Arizona?"

"He was in Phoenix last time I heard. I told Jill we'd make some calls this weekend."

"Then you'll help her."

"Of course. I wouldn't put her through this alone. I wouldn't trust *him* alone with her."

"And you'll go out there with her?"

Chris nodded.

"It'll be the first time you've seen him since—"

She nodded again.

"Think you'll feel anything?"

Even if she hadn't sensed his unsureness, she would have said the same thing. "I'll feel exactly what I felt when he told me he didn't know if the baby was his and walked away—anger, frustration and fear." She touched Gideon's lean cheek and said softly. "But you have nothing to worry about. He won't interest me in the least.''

"Maybe I could come with you."

"That might put more pressure on Jill."

"Then maybe I can help you find him. I have a friend who lives out there—" He stopped when she shook her head. "Why not? It might speed things up."

"It might tell her you're trying to get rid of her."

Gideon couldn't believe his ears. "Are you kidding? She knows better than that!" But Chris was wearing a strange expression. "But maybe you don't." He swore against the anguish that shot through him. "When will you accept the fact that I want her with us?"

"Some men wouldn't."

"I'm not some men," he barked.

"You've been a bachelor for a long time. It's one thing to live with a woman, another to suddenly inherit her teenage daughter."

He was hurt. "Have I ever complained? Have I ever suggested, even in the slightest way, that I didn't want her around?"

"I remember a few very frustrating times—"

"Yeah, I remember them, too, and I'd have felt that frustration whether it was Jill we had to behave for or a child that you and I had ourselves, but that doesn't mean I don't want her. Or them. I want kids, Chris. We're using birth control because we're not married yet, and because we want you to have a choice this time, but I do want kids. I want them for us, and I want them for Jill. She'd love some brothers and sisters. She told me so.''

''She did?''

He nodded. ''When we were out shopping the other week. She said that you were a great mother, and that she hoped you'd have some children so you'd have someone to take care of when she went off to school.''

Chris's face fell. ''Off to school. College.''

''She is going.''

''I know. It's creeping up so fast.'' Closing her eyes, she made a small, helpless sound. ''Why do things have to change?'' It was the question she'd been asking herself over and over again.

Gideon had never pretended to be a philosopher. All he could do was to speak from the heart. ''Because we grow. We move on to things that are even better. Hey, listen, I know it's scary. Change always is. But just think—if Jill goes to see Brant and gets him out of her system, you won't have to worry about that anymore. Then, if you and I get married and have a few kids who adore Jill so much that they raise holy hell when she goes off to college, you'll have something else to think about besides an empty nest.''

''Empty nest—hah. From the sounds of it, you've got the nest so full, there may not be room for any of us to breathe!''

''Not to worry,'' was his smug response. ''I'm a builder. I'll enlarge the nest.'' He doubted it was the time or place, still he couldn't resist pressing his point. ''So, what do you think?''

''About what?''

"Having kids."

"What about my career?"

"You'll cut back a few hours. So will I. Between the two of us, we'll handle things." He paused, wanting to believe but afraid to. "Are you considering it?"

"Not now. All I can do now is to get through this thing with Jill and Brant."

"You'll get through it," he said. Ducking his head, he kissed her on the lips. When she didn't resist, he did it again, more persuasively this time, more deeply. Just as he felt the beginning of her response, he tore his mouth away. "Do you still blame me for Jill wanting to go?"

Closing her eyes against his chin, Chris whispered, "How can I blame you for anything when you kiss me that way?"

"Are you gonna shut me out again?"

"You'll only barge your way back in."

"How about dinner tonight?"

"Goin' for broke, hmm?"

"Damn right."

She opened her eyes and slowly met his. "Okay, but I have to be home early. Jill will be back from her friend's at nine, and I want to be there."

Understanding why, Gideon nodded.

Chris studied his face, feature by handsome feature, for another minute before wrapping her arms around his neck. "Thank you, Gideon."

"For what?"

"Being my friend."

"My pleasure."

She was silent for a minute, thinking about how very much she did love him and how, surprisingly, she was coming to depend on him. She hadn't wanted that at all, but just then, she wasn't sorry. Having someone to lean on was a luxury. Sure, she had her parents and brothers, but it wasn't the same. Gideon was a man. Her man. Holding on to him, being held in return, was the nicest thing that had happened to her in two whole days.

10

Gideon would have liked to have been there when Chris made the call to Brant Conway. He knew the call was, in some respects, a pivotal point in her life, and he wanted to be part of it. But he also knew how worried she was about Jill. He could appreciate how sensitive a time it was for her. The last thing he wanted was to complicate things with his presence.

That didn't mean he couldn't keep in close contact by phone. He wanted to give Chris support, to show her that he could listen and comfort, even absorb her anger and frustration.

Actually, there was far less anger and frustration than he expected. When she finally contacted Brant, then called to tell him about it, she was more tired than anything else.

"It was so easy," she said in a quiet voice, talking in the privacy of her bedroom after Jill had finally gone to sleep. "One call to Directory Assistance did it. He's still living in Phoenix, still selling real estate."

Gideon wanted to know everything. "Who talked, you or Jill?"

"Me," Chris said emphatically. "Jill wanted to do it, but I put my foot down. Can you imagine what she'd have felt if he'd denied he was her father?"

"Did he?"

"I didn't give him a chance. He was slightly stunned when I told him my name. He never expected to hear from me. So I had an advantage to start with, and I pressed it. I told him Jill was fifteen, that she looked just like him, and that she wanted to see him. I told him we'd be flying out during April vacation."

"What'd he say?"

"He stammered a little. Then he said that he had a wife and two little boys, and that Jill's showing up out of nowhere would upset them."

"The bastard," Gideon muttered.

"Uh-huh."

"So what'd you say?"

"I wanted to tell him that he was the scum of the earth and the last person I wanted my daughter to see, but Jill was sitting right there beside me, hanging on my every word. So I just repeated what I'd said, that she wanted to see him. I made it sound as if we were coming whether he liked it or not. I suggested that we would stay in a hotel and that he could visit with her there."

"Did he agree?"

"Reluctantly. He must have figured that he had no choice. We'd gotten his phone number. We could get his address. I doubt he wants us showing up at his house and surprising the wife and kids."

Gideon heard bitterness at the last. "Does it bother you—the idea that he has a family?"

"I kind of figured he did," Chris said. She didn't have to think long about her feelings on that score. "I'm not personally bothered in the least. I wouldn't want the creep if he was presented to me on a silver platter. What does bother me is that he's given legitimacy to two other children, while denying it to Jill."

"She's better off without him. You know that."

"I do." Chris sighed. "I just wish she did."

"She will. Give her time." His thoughts jumped ahead. "When will you go?"

"A week from Monday. We'll come back Wednesday. That leaves Tuesday to see Brant."

Gideon remembered the trips he'd made to see his mother, when he'd flown west, visited and flown home. Years later, he wished he'd taken greater advantage of the cross-country flight. "What about seeing the Southwest? I hear it's beautiful. Maybe you could kind of make it a treat for Jill. I mean, since you're going so far—"

"I thought of doing that, and one part of me would like to. The other part doesn't think it would be so good."

"Why not?"

"Two reasons." She really had thought it out. "First, I don't want her directly associating Brant with that part of the country. I'd rather she see it at a separate time."

"The second reason?"

"You," Chris said softly. "I'd rather not be away from here so long."

Gideon swore. "Damn it, Chris, how can you say something like that on the phone, when I can't hold you or kiss you or love you?" The mere thought of doing all that made his body tighten.

"You asked."

"Right." And since she was in an answering mode, he went for it all. "You do love me, don't you?"

She sighed. "Yes, Gideon, I do love you."

"Since when?"

"I don't know since when. I knew I was in trouble way back at the beginning when you bothered me so much. You kept zinging me with these little darts. I think they had some kind of potion on them."

"Will you marry me?"

"Uh-huh."

"When?"

"Someday."

"'Someday'? What's *that* supposed to mean?"

"I have to get this business with Jill straightened out first."

Gideon's mind started working fast. "Okay. This is April. The trip's comin' right up. Can we plan on a wedding in May?"

"We can't plan on *anything*. We'll have to take it day by day."

"But you will marry me?" He was so desperate for it he'd even wear a tux if she asked. "Marry me, Chris?"

"Yes." And she knew she would. With his enthusiasm, his sense of humor, adventure and compassion, his gentleness and his fire, he had become a vital part of her life. "I do love you," she said, knowing he wanted to hear the words again, knowing he deserved them.

"Ahh." He let out his breath and grinned. "You've just made me a very happy man, Christine Gillette. Horny, but happy."

Both feelings persisted through the next day, which was Saturday. The first was remedied that night, in the coziness of Chris's bed, while Jill was at a movie with friends. The second just grew.

Sunday night, though, Chris phoned him in a state of restrained panic. Her sentences were short and fast, her voice higher than usual. "Brant called a little while ago. Jill answered the phone. I was in the bath. You won't believe what he did, Gideon! I still can't believe it myself! He is such a snake," she hissed, "such a snake!"

"Shh." His heart was pounding, but he said, "Take it slow, honey. Tell me."

"Instead of waiting until I could get to the phone, he talked directly to her. He said that his parents want her to stay with them. Her. Not me. Just her. He said that I shouldn't even bother coming out, that he would meet the plane himself and then deliver Jill to her grandparents." She nearly choked on the words. "Her grandparents. Well, at least he acknowledges that she's his, but to call those people her grandparents when they haven't given any more of a damn than he has all these years—"

"Chris, shh, Chris. Maybe they didn't know."

She was trembling, though whether from anger or fear she didn't know. "That's beside the point. They don't have any right to her. *He* doesn't have any right to her. She's mine. He should have made his plans through *me*." She caught in a livid breath. "Can you believe the *audacity* of the man to go over my head that way?"

"You'll tell him no."

"That's what I told Jill, and she got really upset. She said that he sounded nice, that she was old enough to travel alone, and that that was what she'd been planning to do in the first place." Her voice dropped to a desperate whisper. Though she had her door shut, she didn't want to take the chance that Jill might hear. "But how can I *let* her, Gideon? How can I let her fly all that way alone, then face a man who—for all I know—is strange or sadistic? It's been more than fifteen years since I've seen him. We were kids ourselves. I have no idea what kind of person he's become."

"Did you know his parents?"

"I met them once or twice, but that was all." She could barely picture what they looked like. "What should I do, Gideon? This is my *baby*."

Gideon was silent for a bit. She wanted his opinion, but he was still a fledgling, as parents went. Talk about trial by fire...

"Have you run this by your parents?"

"Not yet. I want to know what *you* think."

"I think," he said slowly, "that you need more information before you can make any kind of judgment."

"Sure, I do," she returned facetiously. "I need a complete dossier on the man, but there's no way I can get that without hiring an investigator, and I refuse to do that! I shouldn't have to pay the money, and we don't have the time."

"I have a friend in Phoenix," Gideon reminded her. "He's a builder there. If he hasn't run across Conway himself, he's bound to know people who have. Let me call him. He may be able to tell us something about what kind of person he is."

"What kind of person is your friend?"

"A trustworthy one."

Chris wasn't about to look a gift horse in the mouth. She agreed to let Gideon do it and was grateful for his offer. Late the next day, he called with the information his friend had provided.

"According to Paul, Brant Conway has made a good name for himself. He's successful in his field, has some dough, lives in a nice house in Scottsdale. He isn't exactly a fixture in high society but he's respected and liked. His parents live in Scottsdale, too. They all do well for themselves."

Chris had mixed feelings about that. She was pleased for Jill, not so pleased for herself. If the report had come back in any way negative, she might have been able to cancel the trip. It looked as though she didn't have any grounds for that.

"And your friend is reliable?" she asked.

"'Fraid so," Gideon answered.

She paused. "Do you think I should let her go?"

"I think that if you don't, Jill may resent it. The fact is that if she wants to go, she'll go anyway, whether it's now or later. It would be awful if your refusal put a wedge between you. I think you have to trust that you've raised her the right way, and that she'll be able to take care of herself and know to call if there's any problem."

That was pretty much what Chris's parents had said when she'd talked it over with them that morning. She had wanted to argue then, just as she wanted to argue now, but she knew that they were all right. Jill wasn't a small child. She would be met at the airport and cared for by her grandparents, who possibly felt far more for her than Brant. Most importantly, Jill had a sane head on her shoulders. If something went wrong, she would know to get herself to the nearest phone.

Heart in her mouth, Chris saw Jill off for Phoenix on the Monday of her school vacation. Brant had suggested that she stay until Friday—another suggestion that Chris resented but that she was helpless to deny.

She did deny Gideon the chance of going to the airport. "My folks want to drive us. Any more people and it'll be a major production." But he was on the phone with her as soon as she returned to the office, and when she got home that night, he was waiting with his overnight bag in the bedroom.

Deliberately that first night, he didn't make love to her. Sex wasn't the reason he'd come. He was there to be with her, to hold her, to talk through her unease and help her pass the time until she heard from Jill.

Jill called late Monday night to say that the flight was fine, that Brant's parents' house was pretty and that Brant had been nice. Chris would have been reassured if she felt that Jill had been making the call in private. She could tell from the conversation, though, that Jill wasn't alone.

"Do you think she's hiding something?" Chris asked Gideon fearfully the minute they'd hung up.

Gideon had no way of knowing that, but he felt he had a handle on Jill. "Your daughter is no wilting violet. If there's something she wanted to tell you but couldn't, she'll find another time to call."

"What if they won't let her?"

"She'll find a way." Taking her in his arms, he hugged her tightly. "Chris, don't expect the worst. You have no reason to believe that Brant's parents are anything but lovely people just discovering a very beautiful granddaughter. Jill sounded well. She's doing fine."

The call that came from Phoenix Tuesday night was like the first, sweet and correct. This one held news on the weather, which was warm, the desert, which was in bloom, and her grandparents' swimming pool, which was "radical."

"See?" Gideon said when they hung up the phone this time. "She's being treated very well." He said it as much for Chris's benefit as for his own. Living with

Chris, being part of her daily life, anticipating what it would be like when they married, he was approaching things from a new angle. He missed Jill. In truth, though he kept telling himself there was no cause, he was worried, too. "If they took her on a Jeep tour of the desert, they're obviously making an effort to show her the sights."

"Brant's parents are," Chris conceded reluctantly. "She doesn't say much about Brant."

"Maybe that's just as well. If she's seen him, her curiosity is satisfied. If there's going to be any kind of continuing relationship, let it be with his parents."

Chris couldn't imagine going through the hell of that kind of visit several times a year, but she knew Gideon was right. Grandparents were often kinder than parents. She supposed, if she was looking to the positive, she should be grateful they were there.

Clinging to that thought, she calmed herself some, enough so that she didn't fall apart when Jill called on Wednesday night sounding like she wanted to cry.

"What's wrong, baby?" she said softly. She could recognize throat-tight talk when she heard it, particularly in the daughter she knew so well.

After an agonizing minute, Jill said, "I miss you."

Tears came to Chris's eyes. "Oh, sweetheart, sweetheart, I miss you, too." She clutched Gideon's hand, wishing Jill had one as strong to hold. "Aren't you having a good time?"

Jill's voice fell to a murmur. "It's okay. But they're strangers. I don't think they knew I existed at all until he told them, after you called. They don't know what to do with me." Her murmur caught. "I wish you were here. You were right. We should have both come. We could have stayed at a hotel. Then it wouldn't have been so awkward."

Chris swallowed her tears. "Day after tomorrow you'll be home."

"I wish I was now."

"Hang in there, sweetheart. We'll be at the airport Friday to pick you up."

"Gideon, too?"

"Yeah. He misses you."

"Mom?"

"What?"

The murmur dropped to a whisper. "I'm glad you didn't marry Brant. Gideon's so much better."

"Oh, honey." Pressing her hands to her lips, Chris looked at Gideon through a pool of tears.

"What?" he whispered. He'd about had it with sitting still, trying to catch the gist of the conversation from Chris's short words and now her tears. Clearly Jill was upset. He wanted to snatch the phone away and talk to her himself, only he didn't know how appropriate it was. Chris might think he was butting in where he didn't belong, and though *he* knew he belonged there, he didn't know if Chris saw that yet.

In place of an answer, Chris transferred her fingers from her lips to his. To Jill, she said a soft, "Thanks, honey. Maybe you'll tell him that when you get home."

"I sure will," Jill said, sounding better.

"Are you okay, now?"

"I think so."

"If you want to call again, just call."

"I will."

"Don't forget."

"I won't."

"Bye-bye, sweetheart. I love you."

"I love you, too, Mom. Bye."

Chris hung up the phone, all the while looking at Gideon with eyes still moist with tears. "She's special."

"Damn it, I know that," Gideon said crossly. He was feeling shut out. "What's wrong out there?"

"She's lonesome. They're not what she's used to. She wished I'd gone with her."

Gideon stared at her for another minute before snatching up the phone. By the time he was done with his call, he was feeling defiant. "That's what I should have done in the first place," he told Chris.

Her mouth was agape and had been since the start of his call. "You made reservations to fly to Phoenix?"

"For two." His finger wagged between them. "You and me. I can't take this sitting around, worrying about her. We're leaving at dawn tomorrow, we'll be there by noon, so we'll have the rest of the day to pack her up and take her off and decide what we want to do for the rest of the week. I vote for the Grand Canyon. I've never been there. Jill will love it. And there are some great places to see along the way. Then we can fly home on Sunday."

Chris couldn't believe what he'd done. More than that, she couldn't believe the feeling she saw in his eyes. "But—but you have work," was all she could manage to say.

"I have Johnny, and even if I didn't, work'll wait. We're right on schedule, even a little ahead at the Rise, which is the one project I've been worried about. I could use a vacation."

"You took one in February."

"So did most of my men, so it didn't matter then, and we're only talking two days here. I deserve it." Scowling, he stuck his hands on his hips. "I should have suggested this when the plans were first made. It would have made things a whole lot more enjoyable for all of us. But I was afraid to say anything, because Jill's not my daughter, she's yours, and I'm not even your husband. But damn it, if we're gonna be a family, we're gonna be a family. That means good times and bad. It means we stick together. It means we share things." He held up a hand and arched a brow in warning. "Now, if that's not what you want, I think you'd better tell me right away, because if it isn't, I'm not the guy for you. If it is, let's get married—now. I have no intention of sitting at home by myself for the next three years until Jill goes off to college and you decide you're lonesome. Either you want me or you don't. Either you love me, or you don't. I've waited almost forty years for a woman as warm and giving and bright and sweet and sexy as you, and I can't wait any longer. I just can't." He took a deep breath. "So, what'll it be, Chris? Do we get married, or do we call the whole thing off?''

Chris eyed him askance. "You're giving me an ultimatum?''

"That's right," he said, returning his hand to his hip. "Not only that, but I want an answer now. And don't tell me that I'm rushing you or pressuring you, because you either feel it here—" he knocked a fist to his heart "—or you don't. If you love me, and you know I love you, we'll be able to handle anything that comes up with Jill." His face went beseeching. "Don't you see, it's the love that counts?''

At that moment, Chris would have had to be blind not to see, ignorant not to know, heartless not to feel. Gideon Lowe, master-builder, macho flirt, notorious bachelor, rabid Celtics fan, was also a man of sensitivity and insight. If she'd ever wanted a stepfather for Jill, she couldn't have asked for a better one. But Gideon was more, even than that. Far more. He was kind and caring and generous. Yes, he'd upset the applecart of her life, but in such a way that the apples would never taste as sweet without him. When she was with him, she felt the kind of wholeness she'd seen in her parents. If she'd ever wanted a lover, she couldn't have asked for a better one. And if she'd ever wanted a husband . . .

"Yes," she said softly, and went to him. "I see. I do see." She slipped her arms around his neck, leaning into him in such a way that their physical fit was as perfect as everything else. "The love's there. Let's do it."

Gideon's eyes lit up in the endearingly naughty way that she loved. "*Do* it?"

She grinned, feeling, with the commitment, suddenly happier and more light-headed than she ever had before. "Get married." She paused. Her grin tilted. "And the other, too."

He didn't need to hear any more. Scooping her up in his arms, he made for the stairs.

"Put me down, Gideon Lowe," she cried, laughing. "Put me down. I can walk. This is embarrassing."

He didn't miss a step. "Embarrassing? It's supposed to be romantic."

"It's totally tough and macho."

He did stop then, just shy of the top step, and met her gaze. "The irony of that is really too much."

"What irony?"

"Crosslyn Rise. I went into the project to shake the image."

"What image?"

"Brawn versus brain. And here I am, carting you off to bed like the best of my big-rig buddies." His grin grew wicked. "Know something?" When she shook her head, he said, "This is the *smartest* damn thing I've ever done in my life." Still grinning, he took the last step.

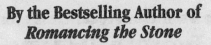

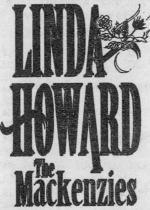
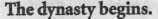